"Sequil"

Or Things Whitch Aint Finished in the First

By Henry A. Shute

"Sequil"

Or Things Whitch Aint Finished in the First

By Henry A. Shute

Start Publishing PD LLC

Manufactured in the United States of America

Cover art: Shutterstock/Taisiya Kozorez

Cover design: Jennifer Do

10 9 8 7 6 5 4 3 2 1

ISBN 979-8-8809-1136-3

Sept. 7, 186- Gosh, what do you think, last nite father and mother and me and Keene and Cele and aunt Sarah was sitting at supper when father, he sed i am a going to read your diry tonite. Gosh i was scart for i hadent wrote ennything in it for a long time. so after supper i went over to mister Watsons and asked him if he dident want to see father and he sed he wood and i went home and told father mister Watson wanted him to come over jest as quick as he cood and father went over. i knew father woodent ever think of it agen. father and mister Watson Beanys father set and talked about what they usted to do and father sed do you remember Wats that time you and Bill Yung and Brad Purinton and Jack Fog went down to, and then he saw me and Beany lissening and he sed, you boys run away and he giv me 5 cents and me and Beany went over to old Si Smiths for some goozberies but i have got to wright that old diry some more whitch is pretty tuf, i have forgot whether it was brite and fair sence i wrote my last diry or not, but ennyway it is brite and fair today. Lots of things have hapened sense i wrote my last diry. Beanys father is a poliseman now and Beany feels prety big. Beany hadent better say mutch to me ennyway. the stewdcats have come back and they has been lots of fites. Scotty Briggam licked 2 stewdcats in one day. one day me and Pewt and Beany was standing in frunt of the libary and 2 stewdcats went in and Pewt threw a peace of dry mud and it hit the stewdcat rite in the neck and bust and went down his coller and he see us laffin and he walked rite out to where we was standing and he sed sorter sisy like whitch of you boys throwd that, and Pewt sed jest like him, if you are so smart you had better find out, and he grabed Pewt and throwd him rite in the guter and roled him round in the mud and hit him 3 good bats in the ear. me and Beany run and Pewt he was mad becaus we dident pich in and help him, but lots of times me and Beany has got licked and Pewt never helped us. i told Father about it and he sed he was glad of it and he wished the stewdcats had licked me and Beany two.

Sept. 8, 186- brite and fair. the band played tonite downtown. we all went down but mother and aunt Sarah and the baby and Franky and Georgie and Annie who was all two little except mother and aunt Sarah who had to stop and take care of them. the band played splendid and Fatty Walker jest pounded the base drum as hard as he cood. most of the fellers run round and played tag and hollered but i set still. i cant see how fellers can run round and holler when a band plays. they tried to pull me out of my seet but i giv Beany a good punch. when we came home mother asked if i had behaived and father sed i set there jest like a old potato. he sed i dident know much ennytime but when i herd music i dident know ennything.

Sept. 9, 186- Will Simpkins is coming to visit us. he is my cuzon and is older then i am and every time he comes he licks me. i dont dass to tell becaus he is company. so this time i am going to get Gim Erly or Tady Finton to lick him. he is coming next Saterday. he lives in a city and wears a neckti every day and feels prety big and says i am a countryman.

I see Gim Erly today and he says he will lick time out of Will for a nife and a slingshot. i had lost my nife so i told Beany and he sed he wood give Gim his nife if he wood let him see the fite. Will licked Beany last summer and Beany aint forgot it. then i dident have enny slingshot and so i told Fatty and Fatty he sed he wood give Gim his slingshot if he cood see the fite. it seemed kinder mean not to tell Pewt, so i told Pewt and he sed he would give me his fathers pigs bladder when it was killed if i wood let him see the fite, that makes 2 bladders i am going to have this fall. Oliver Lane is going to give me his, they will make bully footballs. i gess i can get Potter to give me a leest flycatches egg if i will let him see the fite.

Sept. 10. Brite and fair. Will Simpkins is coming tomorrow. i bet he will wish he hadent after Gim Erly gives him that licking. Potter gave me a red wing blackbirds egg and a chippys egg and 2 blewjays wings to see the fite.

Sept. 11. Brite and fair. it was the best fite i have seen since Cris Staples licked Charlie Clark you had aught to have seen it. Will came this morning he was all dressed up and had his shoes blacked. i knew that wood make Gim want to lick him. i felt kinder mean when he came becaus he seamed glad to see me, and mother sed i hope you boys will have a real nice time together, and i sed i gess we will. so after dinner i asked him to go over to Beanys and we went over and Gim was there and Potter and Pewt and Fatty and Billy Swett came with Fatty and he wispered he wood giv me a whailbone bow. Gim sed to me easy have you got them things and i sed yes and Gim sed no fooling and i sed hope to die and i crosed my throte and i sed you have got to lick him first and he sed he wood lick him. so we went over in the high school yard to play prisners bass. well prety soon Gim sed Will cheeted, and Will said he dident, and Gim sed do you mean to call me a lier and Will sed he dident cheet and Gim sed he wood giv him a paist on the nose, and Will sed he want man enuf and Gim scrached a line in the dirt and told Will not to dass to step over it and then Will put a chip on his sholeder and told Gim not to dass to nock it off and Will sed if he hit Gim he wood nock him so far he woodent come down at all and Gim sed if he hit him there woodent be ennything left of him but a red neckti, and Will told Gim he was a freckled faced mick and Gim told Will he was a curly haired nigger and just then Fatty give Will a push rite into Gim and they went at it and Gim licked time out of Will and got him down and lammed him until he hollered enuf. then Will he went home balling and i had to go two and when we got home mother sed it was a shame and she wood tell father when he got home. when father got home mother told him and sed it was a shame that Willy, she calls him Willy, i am glad my name aint Willy, i had rather be called Skinny or Polelegs or Plupy then Willy, well she sed it was a shame that Willy coodent play with me without having that dredful Erly boy fiting him and she wanted father to go up to Mr. Tucks where Gim lives and tell him about it. Well father sed boys always fit and she mustent wurry about it he gessed Willy wood get over it. but he told me not to ask Gim Erly down here agen. so after supper when i had to go for the yeest i ran up to Gims and giv him the nife and the slingshot and told him not to tell.

Sept. 12. Brite and fair. Will has got a black eye and a scrached nose. Nellie has got well and we had a ride today after church and i let Will drive. in the afternoon Beany and Pewt came over and we had a shooting mach with the whailbone bow behind the barn. i told Beany and Pewt not to tell for if they did father woodent let us go together agen. Fatty and Potter and Billy Swett wont tell ether.

Sept. 13, 186- Brite and fair. today we had a good time. mother let me invite Beany and Pewt and Nipper Brown to supper for company for Will. Pewt coodent come becaus he shot one of his fathers hens with his arrow rifle jest like i shot my hen whitch was eating eggs and Mister Purinton Pewts father woodent let him come. i gess if father had been at home for supper i wood have got a licking but he dident get home til the 7 oh clock train. well we had been raising time up in my room and when we went down to supper i pulled a chair out when Nipper went to set down and he set rite down on the floor bang and grabed the table cloth and pulled of his plate and cup and sauser and Beanys sauser and they came rite down on his head and broak to smash. Nipper was scart but mother picked him up and said he needent wurry for she dident care for the dishes and asked him if he was hurt and said it was my falt and she told me i had aught to be ashamed and I hadent aught to have company if i dident know how to treet them. she dident send me to bed becaus she had to be polite to Beany and Nipper and so i was all rite, after supper we played domminoes til the nine oh clock bell rang and then Beany and Nipper went home.

Sept. 14. Brite and fair. Will went home to-day i was sorry he went, we had a good time and i never knew him to be such a good feller before. i gess it did him good to get a lickin. father says it always does me good to get a good lickin. before he went he got me to throw a ball easy at him and he let it hit him in the eye so he cood tell his folks that a ball hit him in the eye, so he wood not have to tell a lie to his father about his black eye. a feller feels a good deal better when he doesent have to lie to his folks. when i usted to hook in swiming i usted to stick my head in the rane water barril so I cood tell father how i wet my hair. i dident like to do it sometimes becaus the barril was full of little wigglers but i had ruther do that then have to tell a lie, ennyway i gess all the wigglers that got into my hair died becaus they never bit me. father says they turn into musketers.

Sept. 15, 186- Brite and fair. i forgot to say that i giv Will the whailbone bow that Billy Swett giv me to see the fite. he was glad to get it i tell you, and he sed i was the best feller he knew. i told him when he came here agen we wood have some more fun. mother gave him 25 cents and gave me ten cents for being so good to him. me and Pewt and Beany had some goozeberies down to old Si Smiths. father told me one time i cood have a football, so i asked him tonite and he sed i dident desirve ennything, that i had caused him a good deal of truble, ennyway i am going to have 2 bladders.

Sept. 16. Clowdy but no rane. Beany and Ticky Moses got fiting at resess today. we was playing 2 old cat and we was chewsing sides, and Beany and Ticky was chewsing and the way they did it was this. Beany he throwed the bat at Ticky and Ticky he cought it about half way down, and then Beany he put his hand above Tickys and Ticky he put his above Beanys, and so on til when they came to the end of the bat the last one whitch had his hand on has the first choice and no fudging, only he has got to swing the bat around his head 3 times and throw it 3 times as far as he can gump. well Beany he had the last hand on the bat and he cood jest get hold of it a little and when he swung it round his head it sliped and hit Ticky on his head, and he piched into Beany and jest as they was fiting good the bell rang. that is jest the way. something always stops the good fites. i bet on Beany.

Sept. 17. Brite and fair. the stewdcats have got back long ago— i forgot to wright that in. they are some new fellers not enny biger then i am. Honey Donovan licked one of them easy and made him ball like a baby. Chitter Robinson and a stewdcat named Hall had a fite on the Plains and neether licked. they fit until they was tired out, and Darlinton a big stewdcat came up and stoped them. they aint much fun in going to school now. all the girls go to school in the libary bilding and they is nobody but fellers in the grammer school. i tell you it is pretty loansom. we fellers dont care mutch if they miss in there lessons.

Sept. 18. Brite and fair. after school today me and Beany and Fatty and Nibby and Lees Moses and Whacker went home by the libary building, when the girls came out they dident pay enny attension to us becaus the high school fellers was there. perhaps they will want to slide on our sleds next winter and then i gess they will find out something.

Sept. 19, 186- Brite and fair. went to church in the morning and to sunday school in the afternoon. i have got a new pair of britches. old Missis Stickny made them out of a old pair of fathers. they wasent very old becaus they was made out of the same blew coat that father had when he was going to make his speach when old Dirgin put me out of the town hall. father sed he wood never ware them britches ennymore. they was too tite, and his new boots was too tite two, and so he giv them to me, only i cood have the britches made smaler and i coodent have the boots made smaler so i will have to wate a long time before i cood ware the boots. well after sunday school me and Bug and Cawcaw and Pile Wood went down to the dam. they are having the dam fixed and the water is auful low, rite below the dam they was some big pikerel in a place where they coodent get out. well we took off our shues and stockings and begun to wade in after them and they wood dart round lively and we got pretty well spatered, and than i fell rite down and got wet soping. after that i went rite in and we got 12 big pikerel and we had 3 apeace. so i went home and i was afraid i wood get a licking and i did two, for when i came in father said where in thunder have you been and i told him and said here are some good pikerel for supper and he said i will atend to you sir, and he took me up stairs and gave me a whaling. gosh you bet it hurt. well then he told me to go to bed and said i coodent have my supper, and when i took of my close my legs were all blew and i called mother up to see how i was black and blew and when she came up she said for mersy sakes, the coler has all come out of your pants and you are all chekered blew, so i tride to wash it of, and it woodent come of. so i went to bed and i felt auful hungry and i cood hear them at supper and i could smell beefstake and i almost wished father was ded, and when it was almost dark mother come up with a tray and she had fride one of the pikerel and had some tost and a baked potato and i set up and had a buly supper. mother wasent mad a bit with me but she told me i did rong but she gessed i got my pay for it and i gess i did. mother is jest as good as she can be.

Sept. 20. Brite and fair. the coler hasent gone of my legs yet. tonite father took me down to Erl and Cuts where he got the coat that my britches was made out of and told Erl about it and made me show my legs, and Erl said i gess George, the cloth hadent been spunged, and father said i dont know about the cloth, but he was spunged most damly when he got them. and mister Erl laffed and gave father a pair of new britches, and we went home.

father felt pretty good about it, it dont seam rite, i got a lickin and got my legs all blew and it wont come of, and father got a new pair of britches for nothing. enny way one of these pickerel waid a pound.

Sept. 21. tonite i went over to Beanys. Mister Watson Beanys father was leening his head on his hand and i stumped Beany to pull his elbo out. and we nearly dide laffing to think about it and by and by Beany got up his spunk and pulled his elbo out and his head came rite down on the table and he jumped up and grabed Beany and hit him some good bats and sent him to bed and told me to go home and never come over there ennymore. so i cant go with Beany ennymore. the coler hasent gone out of my legs.

Sept. 22. Rany. the coler has begun to go of my legs.

Sept. 23. Rany as time. we got some soft sope of old man Currier today and the coler is most gone.

Sept. 24. It is all gone now.

Sept. 25. Lubbin Smith and Geen Titcum got fiting at resess today and the bell rung before eether had licked. i bet on Lubbin. i went down for some more pikerel today but the river is two deep now.

Sept. 26. i went to church today. they issent enny fun sundays.

Sept. 27, 186- Brite and fair. today we was playing football at school and Whacker got rooted agenst Colbaths barn and hit his head whack and fell down jest as if he was ded, and old Francis came running out and grabed him up and put water on his head and then he waked up and was all rite but he had a headake.

Sept. 28. Rany as time. father has sold Nelly to old Si Smith. she was lame in her hind leg and when she stands in the stable she holds her hind leg up in the air all the time, and when she goes out she limps auful but after she goes a while she aint lame. so last nite father hiched her up and took me and we drove over to Wire Shaws in Kensington and when we came back he took out the whip and hit her under the belly with it 2 times and you aught to see her go. when we came to old Si Smiths she was going like old Billy Robinsons troter. then father turned round and drove up to Sis and old Si and Shep Hodgden and Gimmy Biddle and Charles Fifield was there and father said this will make jest the horse you want for your store and old Si said she aint biger than a rat and father said i gess she is big enuf to carry out all your lodes unless you put down your price, and then they all laffed at Si, and then Si said she was a puller and father said what do you want Josiar one that you have to push, and then they laffed agen and when father called him Josiar i know Si had better look out for when father calls me Henry i know i am in for a liking. then Si said she is lame in every leg and father said you get in here and drive her and if she goes a lame step i will give her to you, and old Si said to Shep and Gimmy you get in and drive her and they got in and drove off and father said he wood take 50 dolars for her and old Si said he wood give 35 dolars for her and they talked and talked and then Shep and Gimmy came back and said she went all rite and old Si said he wood give father 40 dolars and father said she was worth 50 but as Si was a nabor he wood like to acomodate him. well old Si was counting out the money when he said he bet she was a kicker father said she is kind as a kitten and dont bite or kick dont she Harry and i said she cant kick becaus she always holds up one leg in the stall, and old Si said whats that and i told him how she coodent kick becaus she held up one leg, and then Gimmy and Shep and Charlie Fifield and old Mister Page all laffed and hollered and stamped round and slaped their legs and said that is a good one, and old Si stoped counting his money and swore aufully and father looked auful mad for a minit and then he said she is wirth every cent of 50 dolars and asked Si what he wood give and Si said 15 dolars and they talked and talked and after a while he give father 25 dolars. then we went home and father looked prety mad. i dident know what i had done but when we got home he said Harry you go to bed, so i went up about scart to deth but by and by i crep to the stairs and lissened and he was telling about it to mother and he said if he had sence enuf not to ask me about it he cood had got 15 dolars more out of old Si and he was mad enuf to lick me, and then he began to laff and mother laffed and said it served you jest rite George to try and cheet a old man, and father said Nelly was wirth 50 dolars and the last baril of flour that Si sold him was older then Methooselas gread granfather and he wood have got square with Si if it hadent been for that boy. well mother said you cant whip him for telling the truth and father said thunder no i aint going to lick him but i was mad enuf to. so i felt prety good and crep back to bed.

Sept. 29. Brite and fair. At school today Scotty Briggam jumped over the fence today to get the football and fell on his arm and broke it, and then he went home and came back before school was out with some shingles tied on his arm. Scotty has got some spunk, but i gess Tady Finton can lick him now. Old Francis said 2 axidents in 2 days was too mutch and we mustent play football enny more. so at recess we go behind the school house and have fites. Gim Miller and Ben Rundlet had a good fite, and tomorrow Plug Atherton and Diddly Colket are going to have a fite it is most as much fun to see fites as to play football.

Sept. 30. Brite and fair. we cant have enny more fites. at recess today Plug and Diddly had the best fite i ever saw. they fit all recess and none of us heard the bell and Plug had Diddly down and we were all hollering, paist him Plug and hit him Diddly when old Francis came round the corner and grabed Plug and Diddly. i tell you we all went into school lively and old Francis made Plug and Diddly stand on the platform all the rest of the day with their arms round each others necks and we dident have enny recess in the afternoon. it is pretty tuf. we cant play one old cat becaus old Polly Smith makes a fuss when the ball goes over her fence and we cant play football becaus Scotty broke his arm and Whack got stunted, and we cant fite becaus it is rong to fite. we might jest as well be girls and roll hoop.

Sept. 31, 186- father has got a new pair of hip boots. rany.

Sept. 32. No i ment Oct 2. yesterday was Oct 1, and i got it Sept. 31. went down to Henry Youngs tonite and had my hair cut. he put some auful nise smeling oil on and when i got home they all took turns in smeling of my head.

Oct. 3. i went to Church. Pile Woods sister played the organ she is going to play all time now.

Oct. 4. brite and fair today and yesterday. it was so hot today that me and Chick Chickering went in swiming, the water was cold as time, and we jest ducked our heads and come out lively.

Oct. 5. nothing today. brite and fair. they hasent been enny fites at school for the longest while.

Oct. 6. Keene and Cele has got some new balmoral skirts. they feel prety big.

Oct. 7. Charles Talor was down to the house tonite and kept us all laffing to hear him tell stories about father and Gim Melcher.

Oct. 8. brite and fair. tomorrow me and Beany are going to wirk for Mister Hirvey making ice creem. he is going to give us some and some creem cakes. i missed in school today.

Oct. 9. Brite and fair. i gess i shant forget today very soon. this afternoon we went over to Mister Hirveys and we wirked a long time making ice creem by turning the handles of the buckets and choping up the ice. after we got done he let us come into his saloon and we had to big glasses of pink and yellow mixed and some creemcakes. well after we had et it Beany said less put some pepersass into the rest of the creemcakes. so we did and then we went out and peeked through the window. bimeby a man came in and set down and we saw Mister Hirvey bring in some icecreem and some creemcakes. well we kept peeking and the feller et one creemcake and we heard him say to Mister Hirvey that they were the best creem cakes he ever et and then he took another and took a hog bite out of it and then he jumped up and his eyes buged out and he spit it out and begun to swear and drink water and stamp round and Mister Hirvey said what is the matter and the man spit some more and swore and said they was helfire in the creemcake, and Mister Hirvey looked into it and said some one has put pepersass into it and i bet i know who did it. when i heard him say that i ran round the corner, but Beany waited too long and Mister Hirvey saw him peeking in the window and came out lively. well Beany he ran down into Toles yard as tite as he could go and Mister Hirvey came hipering after him with his white apron on, i dident know he cood run so fast. bimeby he came back holding Beany by the ear. Beany he wood try to hold back until his ear nearly puled of and then he wood come along. well Mister Hirvey snaiked him rite into his saloon and said, did you put that pepersass into my creemcakes, and Beany he said he dident, and Mister Hirvey said i dont want enny lying, and said that Beany and the long leged Shute boy were the last ones in the place and that one of us did it. and Beany he said he dident and he saw me with the pepersass bottel in my hand and Mister Hirvey he said now you have got to eat that creemcake or take a good licking and he took his cane, and held Beany by the coller and said 1 and Beany dident eat it, and then he said 2 and Beany dident eat it and then he said 3 and he hit Beany a auful whack over the legs and Beany hollered like time and held on to his legs, and then Mister Hirvey he said 1 again and Beany dident eat it and he said 2 and Beany dident eat it and jest as he said 3 Beany he grabed it and took a bite and tride to swaller it and i thought i shood die to see him, he spit and clawed at his mouth and he howled and jumped up and down and then he ran over to Charles Toles pump and rensed his mouth and drank out of the horse troth and Mister Hirvey and the man like to dide laffing. i waited till they went in and then i went over to see Beany and when i asked him how he liked the creemcake he said i was a long leged puke. this was one of the times that Beany got cought and i dident.

Oct. 10, 186- Sunday agen. brite and fair it never ranes sunday. father went to church today. he woodent have gone if Keene and Cele hadent been going to sing a duet. i dident want to go becaus i was afraid they wood brake down, but father he said i had got to go and so i went. old mister Blake who sets rite behind us droped his hym book and had to bend way over to pick it up when he set up he hit his bald head a feerful bump agenst the book rack. i nearly laffed out loud and had to hold on to my mouth.

Oct. 11. J. Albert Clark is teaching Keene and Cele a new tune. Keene sings the treble and Cele sings the alto. it is there is a bank where on the wild time grows. at supper tonite i asked what wild time was and aunt Sarah said it must be what father and Gim Melcher used to have. then we all laffed and father told aunt Sarah she was geting so funny that she wood have to wear a kerb bit and a martingail. ennyway it was a good one on father.

Oct. 12. the wind blows feerful. father wants me to lern to sing a tune with Keene and Cele. i dident want to but he said i had got to, so we tried it, and i sung it rong every time. i sung it jest enuf rong to make you feel crepey in your back, and father said if you cant sing better then that you had better shet up. so i shet up.

Oct. 13. clowdy but no rane. Georgie has lerned a new tune. it is i wood i were a fary queen. we are going to have the minister to supper and father is going to make Keene and Cele and Georgie show of. i hate showing of. ennyway i havent got to show of becaus father says i cant sing. i can sing but he dont know it you bet.

Oct. 14. rany and windy. i have got a sore throte. father dident want to have the minister to supper. he said to mother, what in thunder do you want a minister for, and mother said, we must have him becaus he will think it very queer if we dont, only you must be careful not to say or do ennything queer, and father he said he wood keep his eye peeled, but he told mother she must look out for the children.

Oct. 15. still rany, my throte is beter. we are going to have chicking for supper when the minister comes. tonite father brought some new goblets from boston. mother and aunt Sarah wirked all day making pies and cake. then mother let me lite a paper and hold the chickings over it to burn of the little fethers and hairs i like it becaus it smels like thanksgiving only i burnt my hand and it smelt jest like the chicking but i dident like that you bet.

Oct. 16, 186- today the hole town was full of ministers, most of them had long tailed coats and white necktis. Deekon Gooch came down to the house with 2 of them. aunt Sarah was wating in her best dress and when she saw them coming she said Murder Joanna they is 2 of them, what shall we do, and mother said, mercy sakes what will George say. well the bell rung and i went to the door and asked them in and Deekon Gooch said they was Mister Fernald and Mister Robinson, he said they was his brothers. then Deekon he went off and i showed them to the front room up stairs and one of them asked me if i loved the lord and i said yes sir and he said i was a good boy. and then he asked me if i went to church and sunday school and i said yes sir and he asked me what was the tex last sunday and i said i dident know what tex ment and he said what did he prech from and i said he preeched from the pulpit in church and from the platform in sunday school, and Mister Fernald he began to laff and Mister Robinson he said i woodent laff if i was you brother, and then he said what does the minister say after the first prair and i said o yes i know now, he says we will now take up the usual colection and then Mister Fernald laffed again, then Mister Robinson he asked me how many sisters i had and i said 4 and he asked if they went to church and i said Keene and Cele sing in the quire and Georgie goes but Annie and Frankie and the baby was two little and then he asked if father went to church and i said not very often, only when Keene and Cele had to sing a duet, and then he asked me what else he did sundays and i said sometimes he made viniger down celler and sometimes he went over to see John Adams hens or down to Gim Melchers shop or up to Hirum Gilmores, and he said it is very deploorible is it not, brother and Mister Fernald he laffed again and said he gessed he better not ask me any more questions, and perhaps my father woodent like to have me tell all about him, and i said father wasent afrade, and he said he dident give much for ministers ennyway and then Mister Fernald laffed as hard as he cood and Mister Robinson looked mad, then we went down stairs and they shook hands with mother and aunt Sarah and Mister Robinson he set down by aunt Sarah and asked her about the church and prair meetings and why she dident always go and lots of things like that and Mister Fernald he got the baby in his lap and he talked to mother about the children and told us stories and he was jest buly. then bimeby father he came home and he shook hands with them and he said he was glad to see them whitch was a auful lie. then mother said super was ready and we all went in to super and father kept talking and telling stories until mother said George and looked at him, and he shet up and turned red and then Mister Robinson began to pray and all of us kept still but Georgie who began to gigle, and mother looked scowly at her and she shet up two. then father looked at mother and winked and i had to put my hand over my mouth. mother she almost laffed to, and Mister Robinson he kept on praying till bimeby Frankie he said Mama i wish that man wood stop and Mister Fernald he began to coff i bet he wanted to laff. well ennyway Mister Robinson he stoped. then father helped them to chicking and bisket and gelly and coffy and everything and then he helped us and we all begun to eat and bimeby Annie said we have got some napkins tonite, and Frankie said we have got some little plates to put the butter on, and i saw them first, and Annie said we have got some new goblets two, so there, and Frankie run his tung out at Annie and she made up a face at him, and then father told them to stop and they stoped and mother and aunt Sarah turned red and Mister Robinson he looked auful sollum and Mister Fernald looked funny and then he looked at father an begun to laff and father laffed and then we all laffed as hard as we cood, and Mister Fernald he said, dont mind a bit Missis Shute, i have got children of my own, i like Mister Fernald. after super Frankie and Annie were sent to bed and we went into the parlor and father kept us all laffing telling stories, and then Keene and Cele sung now i lay me down to sleep, and there is a bank on whitch the wild time grows, and Cele sung flow gently sweet Afton and Georgie sung i wood i were a fary queen, and then Mister Robinson wanted us to sing a religous song and we sung shall we gather at the river. then they asked me to sing and i said i coodent and father said before he thought, that boy is bedeviled to play a cornet, then Mister Fernald he said let him play it, it wont hurt him, then father begun to tell some more stories and kept us laffin fit to die, and Mister Fernald he said he hadent laffed so much for years, and he said, to mother, Missis Shute i gess you have a prety good natured husband, and she said yes, and father he said he most never got mad and jest then the bell rung, and Keene went to the door and said that Mister Swane the poliseman wanted to see father and father he went to the door and in a minit we herd him swaring and herd him say it is a dam lie Swane and you know it and then Swane went away and father came in and said that someone had ridden horseback over the concreek sidewalk and they tride to lay it on me. Then it was bedtime and Mister Robinson he prayed some more and he prayed for those who took the name of the lord in vane, and then we went to bed.

Oct. 17. Brite and fair. the old ministers has gone. i am glad of it. i liked Mister Fernald but i hated old Robinson. i gess he wont get invited here again. this morning at brekfast he prayed again until the brekfast was most cold and he prayed a good deal about takin the name of the lord in vane and i cood see that mother looked mad but she dident say ennything. bimeby he begun to talk to mother about father having a unfortunate temper, and said his langage was shocking, and Cele she up and said, i gess my father is as good as you are and Keene stuck out her tung and mother sent them away from the table, and then old Robinson he said i am afrade your children are not well brought up, and mother looked rite at him a minit and then she said, i shood feel very badly if my children shood xcept hospitality from another person and crittisise that person to his face, at all events i cannot submit to have my husband or my children crittisized, and Mister Robinson he dident say ennymore you bet. after brekfast they went away, and Mister Fernald he shook hands with us all and he asked mother to let Cele and Keene come down to shake hands and she did. after they had went mother she gave us a peace of mince pie apeace and we all hoorayed for mother. none of us went to church today.

Oct. 18. brite and fair. tonite father borowed Gim Loverings horse and wagun to go riding. Gim said it aught to be greesed, so father asked me to greese the wheals, and then he said i will do it myself, and then i will be sure it will be done rite. so he got the munky rench and the lantern and some lard and went out to greese the wheals, and when he had greesed them he come in and washed his hands and then he went out and told mother not to set up for him and he unhitched the horse and hollered gitap and when the horse started one side of the wagun went down whack and out came father. well he held on to the ranes and stoped the horse and mother said what is the matter, and father said that infernal boy dident screw up the nut and the wheal come of and nearly broke my neck, and as soon as i tie this horse i will give him a good whaling and aunt Sarah said George you greesed the wheals yourself and father said by thunder so i did. then i got the lantern and we looked for the wheal and it was leaning up against the apple tree and father said jest look at that, the wheal ran up to the tree and stoped, and then we hunted round for the nut and we coodent find it and i got down on my nees and father held the lantern, and Cele and Keene came out and hunted and we coodent find it. bimeby father said he could put on the wheal and hold it on till he got back to Gims and he lifted up the ex and i went to put on the wheal and there was the nut all screwed on the ex. father had put on the nut but had forgot to put on the wheal and had left the ex resting on the jack. i gess he hadent better say mutch about me.

Oct. 19. I have got a new box of paper collers.

Oct. 20. brite and fair. this afternoon me and Fatty Melcher wirked all the afternoon puting leafs in old Putty Lowjys barn. old Putty said he wood pay us but when we asked him for our pay he said we cood have all the horse chesnuts we wanted. so we got a baskit and picked it full and went back to Fattys and pluged horse chesnuts at old Puttys cat.

Oct. 21. brite and fair. Skinny Bruce and Ben Rundlet got fiting today. old Bandbox Tomson came in to lern us some music and he left his fiddel in the entry and at resess Ben he put some sope on his bow and when old Bandbox tried to play on it he coodent make a squeak. then old Francis asked every feller in school who done it, and when Ben said he dident know who done it old Francis he up and whaled time out of Ben. i gess old Francis see Ben do it. ennyway after school Skinny he hollered Ben how did you like your licking, and Ben he hollered back Skinny Bruce is a redheaded goose, and Skinny he got mad and paisted Ben one in the eye and Ben he give Skinny a sidewinder and then they fit from first base to Colbaths barn where Whack got stunted and old Polly Smith came out and said if they dident stop fiting she wood go for the polise, and so they stoped. i bet on Skinny.

Oct. 22, 186- brite and fair and most as hot as summer. that was prety mean of old Putty.

Oct. 23. Mary Watson, Beany's sister and Mary Straton whose father chased me and Beany when we broke the gaslite, can run faster then enny of the fellers xcept Tomtit and Arthur Francis.

Oct. 24. i have been sick agen. not very sick but my legs aked ferful. mother says it is becaus i am growin so fast, but i know why, me and Boog Chadwick rassled all yesterday afternoon. ferst i throwed Boog and then Boog throwed me, and when we got through Boog was only 2 throws ahead. we dident get mad at all. ennyway i dident have to go to church.

Oct. 25. tonite we had company to super. Mister and Missis Merill. Frankie did a funny thing. father asked mother for some chese and mother she said they wasent enny, and Frankie he said he knew where they was some and father said all rite Frankie if you can get some i will give you a cent, father he thinks Frankie is auful smart, and so Frankie he climed out of his high chair and ran out into the kitchen and bimeby he came in with 3 little peaces of chese and father he asked him where he got them and he brought in the rat trap. you had just aught to have herd them laff.

Oct. 26. Clowdy but no rane. some folks can eat chese that is all wiggly.

Oct. 27. still clowdy. i cant.

Oct. 28. Beany has got the best little ax i ever saw. his father got it for him to split his kindlins. i wish i had one like it for i have to split my kindlins with a old rusty ax that ways about a tun.

Oct. 29. brite and fair. tonite i went over and helped Beany split kindlins with his new ax. it was jest as easy as ennything.

Oct. 30. brite and fair. old Tom Fifield killed his pig today and give Beany the bladder, and we blew it up with a pipe stem and kicked it for a football after school. Jack Melvin is going to have Micky Kelleys fathers pigs bladder, only he dont kill his pig till most winter. i am going to have Oliver Lanes, and his pig is the bigest in town. i bet his will be as big as the stewdcats big football. all the fellers wish they cood get it.

Oct. 31. cold as time this morning, but i had to go to church jest the same.

Nov. 1. Beany got a licking today for hollering after old Nancy Marble. she went into Beanys house and told Beanys father. i hollered two but father was in boston and she coodent tell him.

Nov. 2. brite and fair. Oliver Lane killed his pig today. it was the bigest pig in town. i had been wating for the bladder ever sense last June and i thought such a big pig aught to have a big bladder, but it was jest the littlest bladder i ever see. i suppose it was so fat inside they wasent enny room for the bladder. Skinny Bruces pigs fathers bladder, no i mean Skinny Bruces fathers pigs bladder was most twice as big.

Nov. 3. Brite and fair. the water in the rane baril was froze over last nite. today i blew up the bladder and dride it in the kitchen. it made a prety good football. Pewt dident give me his fathers pigs bladder that he promised me when i let him see the fite when Gim Erly licked Will Simpkins. you jest wait Pewt and you will see.

Nov. 4. brite and fair. Georgie got sent to bed today and had to stay in bed all the afternoon. mother told her not to tuch a vase that was full of sand to make it heavy. i wanted the sand for my aquarian and so i poored it out. well bimeby Georgie came in and went up to take the vase and it was so lite that when she lifted hard it came up so quick that she went rite over backward and smashed the vase all to bits. mother came running in and found that Georgie wasent hurt, but she howled as loud as she cood so that mother woodent lick her, and so she got sent to bed. mother said it sirved her rite.

Nov. 5. Brite and fair. i have been sick today. i gess i et two much spare rib. when i think of it it makes me sick. so i have been thinking over the poitry about the fellers. some of it is prety good.

Ed Tole fell in a hole and
coodent get out to save his sole

i made that up.

Plupy Shute
is a dirty brute.
and never will fite
if they is a chance to scoot.

Pewt he made that up.

Old Tim Calahan
he was a hell of a man.

Fatty Melcher he made that up.

Frank Hanes aint got enny branes
and dont know enuf to go in when it ranes
Beany he made that up.

Nipper Brown tumbled down
and busted his head and cracked his crown.
i made that up too.
Granvil Miller the barber
went to shave his father
the razer sliped and cut his lip
becaus he forgot the lather.
Skinny Bruce he made that up.

i tell you they is some prety good poits among the fellers. but any feller whitch gets poitry made up about him gets mad.

Nov. 6. brite and fair. Ed Tole can spit further than enny feller in school.

Nov. 7. Keene and Cele are sick in bed and coodent sing today in church. they have feerful headakes. docter Perry came in to see them.

Nov. 8. brite and fair. Keene and Cele and Georgie are all sick now and the docter says it is scarlet fever. they are all up in the front chamber and mother and aunt Sarah take care of them.

Nov. 9. clowdy but no rane. Annie is sick now and i cant go to school ennymore. i like that. so i am making a hen koop.

Nov. 10. Rany today. Beany he hollered over today to find out how Keene and Cele and Georgie and Annie are.

i have got a soar throte but i aint going to tell ennyone about it.

Nov. 11. i had a headake all last nite. i bet i am going to have the fever. Frankie has got it now and mother is afrade the baby is coming down, she asked me how i felt and i said buly.

Nov. 12. old Missis Smith is helping take care of the house and gets the brekfasts and dinners and suppers. today docter Perry he came down stairs and i was setting in a chair and he said what is the matter with you, and i said nothing and he said let me look at your throte, and he made me open my mouth and he looked down in my gozzle and then he said you march upstairs into the hospitle and tell your mother that you are a new pacient and i went up and when mother saw me come in she said well i have been expecting you. then i went down to my room and got my niteshert and i thaught i aught to write this down becaus i might die. people do die of scarlet fever, i wonder if ennyone wood read it if i did die. ennyway father said once that a boy whitch was born to be hung never wood die in enny other way, so i gess i am all rite. ennyway i aint going to wright ennymore till i get well.

*

Jan. 17. brite and fair. i dident die and every one of us got well. Annie had it the wirst and i had it the next wirst and Frankie and the baby want hardly sick any. today is the first time i have been out. Cele and Keene went out last Wensday but i coodent becaus i hadent got done peeling. after folks have the scarlet fever their skin dries up and peels of and if you get cold in the peeling you die every time. i had on my Hoppy Gad boots for the first time today. father brougt them up to show me when i was in bed. i was prety sick and dident know nothing for 2 or 3 days. mother says i was talking about the fellers i knew in Reading. we lived in Reading one year and so i thought i was there i gess and she says i talked of George and Wendal Evans and Puggy Fergerson and Totty Procter and Emma Wallis and Jonny Pike and Ed Harndin and Nelly Minot. i had a fite with Ed Harndin and licked him. when Willy died we came back to Exeter, and she said i talked about Willy to, and everything. we had some fun while we was sick. Cele used to tell stories and we made flyboxes and then when mother was out of the room we wood turn sumersets, and bimeby when we got so that we cood eat apples we used to have one apeace every day and we had to scrape them with a nife and eat the soft part, and when we were geting beter we were auful cross. i gess most every one wood be cross to lose thanksgiving and crismas two, and my berthday, and all the skating and snowbaling. ennyway i havent got to go to school this week.

Jan. 18, 186- buly snowbaling. i went out today a long time, mother told me not to plug snowballs, so i only throwed 2 or 3. i am hungry all the time.

Jan. 19. brite and fair. one of my hens died when i was sick and the rooster frose his comb. it is prety tuf on me.

Jan. 20. i went sliding today on factory hill, it was buly. they wasent hardly ennyone there.

Jan. 21. brite and fair. Whack and Boog have got a duble runner, they made it out of there sleds dart and arrow. it is the fastest duble runner on the hill. i went with them. we beat Pewts duble runner esy. Pewts is biger and Mister Purington Pewts father painted it buly but it cant go as fast or as fur as Whack and Boogs. Pewt was mad becaus we beat him.

Jan. 22. i went to church today. Keene and Cele sung in the quire. Beany kept sticking his head out from behind the organ and making up faces at me to make me laff out loud till the minister spoke to him and he felt prety cheep.

Jan. 23. snowed and raned today both, i had my sled painted today. it is painted black with a gold stripe and Exeter Boy in gold letters on it. Mister Purington Pewts father painted it. i went to school today. nobody got licked.

Jan. 24. clowdy. my sled is most dry enuf to use.

Jan. 25. it misted last nite and frose and today everything was covered with ice it was fun to see people fall down. most everybody fell down. i went sliding on spring street.

Jan. 26. cold as time. i went to school. we are going over colburns in revew and so i can keep up.

Jan. 27. I havent got ennything to wright today xcept that i went to school. John Adams has got a new brama rooster.

Jan. 28. Brite and fair. i licked Ti Crummet today. me and Whack and Fatty Melcher was over on Factory Hill sliding and Ti Crummet and Hirum Mingo and Bobberty Robinson and Dinky Lord came over and i had my sled all new painted, Pewts father painted it and Ti Crummet run his old sled agenst it and nocked of sum of the paint, and i told him to keep his old sled of mine and Ti he said he wood nock sum of the paint of me if i said 2 words more and then he swoar feerfully. i dident say nothing becaus i dident want to fite him, and Hirum Mingo said Plupy says he can lick you Ti and Ti said i can nock hel out of you old spindel legs and i said i dident say so and Ti he swoar sum more so it sort of scart me, well then i was going and Hirum he pushed Ti rite into me and he kicked me in the leg and got hold of my hair and i got the under hold and got him down jest as esy as ennything and then i set on him and lammed him til he holered enuf and then i let him up and he went home balling. i bet he beter not fite me agen.

Jan. 29. Brite and fair. it aint the feller whitch can swear the feerfullest whitch is the best fiter. i went to church and sunday school today.

Jan. 30. Brite and fair. Johnny Kelly can lick enny feller on Court or South Street and he can swear auful two. i gess most of the fellers is scart of him becaus he can swear so. i aint scart of him.

Jan. 31. Rany. not mutch but sum. we was playing snap the whip today and Johnny Kelly was on the end and got snaped rite into a pudel of water and he said i dident hold on and he wood give me a slap in the mug and i said he want man enuf and jest then the bell rang and we had to go in. tomorow he had beter look out i am going to give him one in the eye and then grab for the under hold and get him down and lam him good. i bet he cant fite enny beter then Ti Crummet did, and when i have licked him all the fellers will be afrade of me. i bet he will wish he had never fit with me.

Feb. 1. Brite and Fair. i have got a black eye. this morning i went to school erly and when i got there Johnny Kelly was there and he said now old Plupy longlegs i will fix you and i said pile rite in and we will see and he began to swear wirse then Ti did, and i said if you want a good paist in the gob they is plenty of them rite here if you are man enuf to sale in, and when i said that he come at me so quick that i dident have time to get ready and he hit me in the eye and in the mouth 2 times and got the underhold before i cood and got me down and lammed me till i hollered enuf. then all the fellers holered Plupy got licked Plupy has got a black eye. it was prety mean ennyway. when i got home to dinner mother asked me how i got my eye sore and i said i got it boxing with Johnny Kelly and she said was you fiteing and i said we box every day in school sometimes Beany and Whack and sometimes me and Pewt but today me and Johnny Kelly boxed and he hits to hard and she said she shood think so, and said i had beter box with sum other boy and i gess so two. ennyway i dident lie to her for that wasent lying.

Feb. 2. Brite and fair. i gave Johnny Kelly the core of my apple today. Gosh sum fellers can fite auful and swear auful two.

Feb. 3. Brite and fair. Beany has got a new blew jacket. he felt prety big about it until Pewt took him in the back with a roten apple. Beany staid in all resess a scraping the apple off of his coat. this afternoon he wore his old jacket. but he is going to pay Pewt for that sum way.

Feb. 4. it snowed hard all day all the fellers are whacking cats head on each others back. you take some chork and chork the inside of your hand and your ferst and last finger and then you wet your fingers and make eyes and nose and mouth in your chorky hand and then you wate til a feller comes along and then you lam him one on the back and it makes the funniest cats head on his back you ever see with eyes and nose and mouth and 2 long ears whitch your fingers made. i got 5 on my back today and i got 1 on Beany and 2 on Pewt and 1 on Pop Clark and 1 on Nipper Brown.

Feb. 5. it snowed this morning and we dident go to church i dug some paths and read Billy Bowlegs in the afternoon, after super it snowed again and is snowing now. i bet they will be some deep drifts tomorow.

Feb. 6. brite and fair. it has cleared off. everything was jest as white and they wasent hardly a track in the snow. i had to dig sum paths, and i got up erly and dug a path down the frunt steps and out to the road so father cood get into the hack. Jo Parmer said it was prety tuf slaying. my Hoppy Gad boots have been greesed and they dont leak a bit. me and Pewt and Beany had sum fun diving. we tide scarfs round our heds and necks and div from our steps into a snow drift. and we cood go in way out of sight. we tide our britches down over our boots, it was more fun than diving in the river. after we div one drift all down we tride another, and bimeby Beany he said come on fellers here is a buly drift down by the shed and we went down and Beany said i chuse first dive and he clim up on the shed and said 1 to make ready, 2 to prepare, 3 to be going and 4 to be there, and then he div rite into the swill bucket. it was under the snow and Beany coodent see it, and when he came up he was all swill and he was mad and said i knew it all the time, and he went home and aint going to ever speak to me enny more. i coodent see the old bucket enny more than he cood. it is jest like Beany to get mad at every little thing. i bet he wood laff if i div in the swill bucket.

Feb. 7. Brite and fair. Beany woodent speek to me today. all rite Beany you jest wait and see.

Feb. 8. Brite and fair. it was buly snowballing. we was pluging stewdcats today and Pacer Gooch came along. so we got behind trees and Pewt peeked jest in time to get one rite in the eye. he had aught to know beter than peek out when Pacer is pluging snowballs.

Feb. 9. me and Fatty Melcher are making some arrow rifles down to his shop. we are going hunting for rabbits saterday. brite and fair.

Feb. 10. brite and fair. tonite father brougt a magasine home tonite. it is the young folks. we all wanted it so we took turns. ferst Cele read a story and then i read a story and then Keene, we all read it out loud. Cele read amung the glass blowers. Keene read the story of a bad boy. and i read around the evening lamp. they was all buly stories.

Feb. 11, 186- this afternoon me and Fatty Melcher and Potter Goram went hunting. we had our arrow rifles and Fatty had a ax and Potter a hachet in his belt and i had a nife. we had a buly time. we went up to the eddy and then went across the river on Gilmans side. we saw 2 patriges and 1 rabbit and some blewgays. we dident hit them but we came prety near them. then we bilt a fire and et our donnuts and then we tracked a rabbit into a pile of bushes. when we turned over a log we scart out a field mouse and killed it. tonite Potter came down to the house and we read young yagers.

Feb. 12. it raned hard all day. Keene and Cele had to go to church and so i had to go two. they wasent many there. it ranes now.

Feb. 13. it raned hard all nite. i cood hear it agenst the window and hear the wind blow. it is comfertible to be in bed and hear the rane. only i forgot my kindlings and i had to get up before six oh clock this morning.

Feb. 14. Beany nearly got killed today. he was spliting wood with his new ax and he was standing rite under a closeline. Beany feels prety big about his new ax and he had got so that he can grunt jest like men who chop wood all the time. so Beany he swung the ax over his head and it hit the closeline and bounced rite up in the air and came rite down on Beanys head and he fell down whack and laid there till his father came out and lugged him into the house. they thought he was ded but he wasent. I went over today to see him, he was setting in a rocking chair by the stove with his head rapped up in a towel. i sent Beany a valentine today. he dident send me one but i gess it was because he was sick.

Feb. 15. brite and fair. Beany is better today. i went over and split his kindlings for him.

Feb. 16. brite and fair and buly snowballing. Gimmy Watson, Beanys brother said if Beanys head hadent been jest like the choping block it wood have killed him. Gimmy is mad becaus Beany calls him Gami. He can lick Beany alone and can lick me alone but me and Beany together can lick him.

Feb. 17. they was a fire down on franklin street today and Bob Carter got all squirted over and his close frose to the ladder he was on.

Feb. 18, 186- it snowed today, and then it raned.

Feb. 19. we have vacation in about 2 weeks.

Feb. 20. i shall be glad when spring comes. i wet my feet most every day.

Feb. 21. we are going to have a school xibision at the end of this tirm and old Francis says he is going to give prises to the best scholars. Nipper and Pricilla and all the other good boys are studying hard so as to get the prises. i woodent take one of their prises if they wood give me one. i woodent give 2 cents for their old prises.

Feb. 22. today is Washington's berthday and we can ring the town bell at 1 oh clock and at 5 for a hour. i went down both times and Ed Derbon let us take turns in ringing the bell. only 2 can ring at a time. when me and Fatty Melcher was ringing the bell went over and it pulled us way up to the ceeling. most of the fellers staid out in frunt of the church and pluged snowballs. bimeby some stewdcats came along and we pluged and hit a stewdcat named Lee rite in the back of his head and he said we have stood enuf from these townies and he and Stone and Clifford and Winsor, who was our sunday school teacher until he saw the rooster fite, and Belmont came over the fence and charged us and we pluged as hard as we cood and they pluged two and we ran behind the church and they follered us and jest lammed us and washed Beanys face and rolled Pewt in the wet snow, and jest then Boog and Whack and Puz and Zee Smith came piling in and paisted time out of them and then the stewdcats charged them and throwed Whack in a drift and Zee got one in the back that made him lay down and grunt before he cood get his breth, and then all the stewdcats from Toles house piled out and piched in and they was giving us time when Bozzaris Wadly see the fite and jumped of a load of wood and Pacer and Stuby Gooch and Scotty Briggam and Kibo Marston and Skinny Bruce and Frank Elliott herd us hollering give it to the stewdcats and came running over and then we had jest a buly fite and i tell you the snow balls jest flew and Fatty Gilman got one rite in the eye and Pheby Talor got one rite in the mouth jest as he was hollering stewdcat and it filled his mouth with snow and old Woodbrige Odlin was coming out of the bank and he got one in the leg and one in his old plug hat and it nocked it of and he went over to the hotel and i gess he told old Brown becaus he and Swane and Potsy Dirgin the poliseman came over and made us stop, it was the best snow ball fite i ever saw. we are going to lay for the stewdcats next saterday at the libary. old Bozzaris Wadly was the best fiter we had and nobody knowed he cood fite. when the stewdcats wood charge us he wood not run a bit but wood jest stand and plug and once when Clifford tride to put him over he coodent do it. it was a buly fite.

Feb. 23. Brite and fair. Gosh what do you think i am going to get a prise in school. last nite i had to go down to old Tom Connors store to get some carosene and old Francis was going down town with Perry Molton and they was talking about who was the best fellers in school and who they was going to give the prises. i lissened and old Francis said Potter and Nipper and Pricilla was going to have prises, only he dident call them Potter and Nipper and Pricilla, but Arthur and Jonny and Charlie, then he said they is one boy who is as smart as enny of them only he dont study much and i had to shake him up laitly and he is doing better now, then Perry he said who is it, and old Francis said i gess i wont tell you his name for he may disapoint me, but he lives on Court Street. i tell you it made me feel all tremly. it coodent be Pewt or Beany becaus they miss there lesons most every day and they aint enny other fellers living on Court Street so it must be me, becaus old Francis shook me and Medo Thirsten up day before yesterday and Medo lives on South Street. Gosh wont father be sirprized i nearly got a prise once when Fliperty Flannygan marked my words all rite and i wood have got it if it hadent been for Gimmy Fitsgerald. but this time i am going to get it. i bet the folks will think i am quite a feller.

Feb. 24. Brite and fair. i dident miss in school today. tonite i staid in and studied. Pewt and Beany come round and were mad becaus i woodent come out.

Feb. 25. Rany. i got 9 xamples rite today out of 10, but i missed in speling. it aint often i miss in speling.

Feb. 26. i took a book today to church and studied.

Feb. 27. Rany again. i dident miss in ennything today. i told mother today that i was going to get a prise if i dident disapoint him. so she told father tonite and he said he dident beleive it. he said he had nearly a buchel of prises he got in school and he give them to the fellers to ware in a torchlite percession and they kept them. he said he give all his prise books to the sunday school. he said when he put on all his meddles and walked out they gingled jest like slaybells and glitered so they scart horses. aunt Sarah laffed and said the only prises he wore were black and blew ruler marks that old mister Ellis give him and he got enuf of them to, and she said tell Harry what you left the Academy for, and he said the teachers were down on him becaus he lerned faster than they cood teech, and aunt Sarah said Doctor Sole wood tell a diferent story, and father said that Doctor Sole was a wirthy man but he dident forgive ennyone which was smarter than he was. then father said you talk very strangly Sarah for one of your years and i shall ask the Coart to apoint me as gardeen over you as a person of unsound mind. then father said he had never told ennyone why he left the Academy so suddin, but it was becaus he broak his jaw in 3 places talking Greke to Doctor Sole. well he kept us laffing all the evening and when i went to bed he give me 10 cents so i gess he feels prety good about my prise.

Feb. 28. clowdy but no rane. i only missed in Geogerfy today. Aunt Sarah is going to exibision day to see me get my prise. Keene and Cele are going two. i dont dass to tell Beany. he come over tonite to get me to come out and see him set his dog onto Mister Heads cat and was mad when i told him i had got to study. Beany he says i will get so i cant fite or have enny fun i am geting so good. Beany will get a good punch if he says much.

Mar. 1, 186- brite and fair. father is going to the school exibision.

Mar. 2. Brite and fair. tonite father lerned me a speach to say when old Francis gives me the prise. i dont want to say it but he says i have got to. this is my speach. Mister Francis i thank you very kindly for this beautiful present, whitch i value for the honor whitch has been confered on me, and i trust that i shall so conduck myself that you may never regret it.

Mar. 3. Brite and fair. tomorow is exibision day. today we rehersed. Pricilla sung pulling hard agenst the streem and played the organ. Potter read a composition and Nipper xplaned the sum about the hundred geese the one i never cood do. Good morow farmer with your hundred geese sir i have not a hundred but if i had as many more and half as many more and 2-1/2 geese i shood have a hundred, how many geese had he. well Nipper can do that sum and so he has got to show of. i havent got to do ennything xcept to say my speach when old Francis gives me my prise, whitch is prety good for me.

Mar. 4. Brite and fair. i am not fealing very well tonite. father dident go to boston this morning but staid to home. this morning in school we rehersed for xibision. Pricilla sung and plaid and Nipper rote down the geese sum on the blackboard and rote his name under it jest as good as he cood. i wanted to rite Nipper under it but old Francis wood paist time out of me if he found out who rote it. you aught to hear Pricil play and sing. he sings do your best for one another making life a plesent dream, help a poor and weried brother puling hard agenst the streem, and the old organ goes boom ya, boom ya, boom ya ya ya, that is a prety song for a feller to sing whitch never will give the fellers the core of his apple but always eats it hisself. well this afternoon i put on my best close and my plad neckti and a new paper coller and went to school erly. prety soon the people begun to come in. they was old Perry Molton and old Nat Shute and Gewett Swazie the committy, and old Bil Morrill with his hair curled under behind and Chick Chickerings father and mother and docter Goram, Nippers father and mother and Pricillas father and mother and lots of people and i thought father wasent coming but bimeby he come in with his new britches that he made Erl and Cutts give him and his boots blacked and aunt Sarah and Keene and Cele. Aunt Sarah had got her best earings and her dolman with beeds and Keene and Cele had on their bronze boots and there plad dresses and they got a seet on the platform. Keene and Cele felt prety big becaus they was in the seminary and Aunt Sarah felt prety big becaus she had on her earings and her dolman and father felt prety big becaus i was going to get a prise. well first old Francis said a prayer and everyone bowed there heads and father bowed his two but i saw him peek out under his hand. well then we all sung and Mary Emery plaid the organ. then our class resited and Nipper xplained his sum about the geese and then Potter spoke a peace and then Pricilla plaid and sung his peace. then there was a dialog and then we sung sum more. then old Francis opened his desk and took out a little riting desk and said it had been prety hard to tell whitch was the best scolar becaus they was 3 boys who were so near together. so he would give the riting desk to Arthur Goram and the glass inkstand to Johnny Brown and the stamp colecters book to Charly Hobbs. so when he give them Potter and Nipper and Pricilla stood up and bowd and said thank you. if they had been so smart they aught to have a speach ready. ennyway i had my speach all ready. then old Francis said there was one boy who had grate talents and was a very brite boy but owing to his fondness for play had not done as well as he shood. but he had showed such talent that he aught to be menshioned espesially as he had been studying much better laitly. when old Francis said that aunt Sarah and Keene and Cele set up strate and father tride to look as if he dident know who he meant and i said my speach over soft, to be sure i had it rite. then old Francis said i have selected as a present for this boy a book, and the name of this boy is, and then he stoped a moment and i cood almost hear my heart thumping, and then he said Johnny Chickering. Gosh i had forgotten all about Chick Chickering living on Coart Street. when he said that aunt Sarah and Keene and Cele sat rite back in there chairs and father turned auful red and looked at me as if he wanted to nock my head rite of and then he droped his hat on the floor and it fell of the platform and roled way out under Medo Thirstons seet and then he blew his nose with a auful toot. then old Francis give Chick the book and then he read the names of the 10 next best scolars and my name wasent there eether. and then father looked mad enuf to bust, and Aunt Sarah and Keene and Cele looked prety sick. then we all sung happy school Ah from the never shall our hearts long time be turning, and then school was dismissed. docter Goram and Nippers father and mother and Pricillas father and mother and Chicks father and mother and lots of the people staid to shake hands with old Francis, but father marched rite out and Aunt Sarah and the girls two. well when i got home you aught to have heard father. he said i was the laziest and most wirthless boy there ever was, and i was a disgrace to him and he sent me to bed lively. i dident want the old book ennyway.

Mar. 5. Church today. i dont care.

Mar. 6. Brite and fair. Chick feals prety big about his old book. Ed Tole has got a new game rooster. we are going to throw him over in John Adams yard the first time John lets his bolton gray out. i rode on the hack today all the morning. it is more fun then geting good marks in school. ennyway it is vacation and i am going to raise time. i dont care for a old prise ennyway.

Mar. 7. Brite and fair. i broak a window today on purpose, i dont care.

Mar. 8. Brite and fair. got sent to bed tonite for swearing. all i said was gol darn it. father needent feel so big. i have herd him say wirse things than that. i dont care.

Mar. 9. clowdy but no rane. i dont care if i dident get no prise. Chick needent feel so big. i woodent take his old book ennyway.

Mar. 10. brite and fair. i got fiting with Beany today in his yard. he chased me over to my yard and i turned round suddin and stuck out my arm and my fist hit Beany rite in the eye. you had aught to herd him howl. then mother called me in and sent me to bed. it is prety tuf when a feller cant hit another feller in the eye whitch is chasing him. well ennyway i stamped upstairs to bed and when father came home i knew i shood get a licking. so when father came home i lissened and herd them eating super, and i herd father say where is that boy and mother said i sent him to bed for striking Elly Watson. Elly is Beany you know. and father said whitch licked. and mother said Elly was crying very loud and holding on to his eye, and so i sent Harry to bed and father said if he dident do ennything wirse than licking that Watson boy i wont complane and if he will get up spunk enuf to lick that boy of Brad Puringtons, he ment Pewt, i will give him a treet. then mother said i dont know what is the matter with Harry this vacation. he is cross and impident, and then Keene said i slaped her face yesterday and Cele told Keene it was her falt and she hadent aught to have plaged me, and Keene said she dident and Cele said she did and father said you girls shet up when your mother is talking. then someone shet the door and i dident hear enny more. after super Cele come up in my room with a tray with my super and i set up in bed and et my super and Keene looked into the room and made up a face. after super i heard father talking again and he said i needed a good licking and mother said something was the matter with me and she never knew me to keep cross for a hole week, and father said he wood take it out of me in 2 minits and mother said no she wood talk to me. So bimeby mother come up and i made beleeve i was asleep and mother set down by the bed and said are you asleep Harry, and i said yes before i thought, and then she sorter laffed and began to talk to me and told me how sory it made her feel to see me so cross and doing bad things and she wanted me to be better and not wurry her for she dident feel very well and gosh before i knew it i was balling rite out. well i balled good and she rubed my head and got me a drink of water and i said i wood do beter. then she kissed me and went down and after a while i went to sleep. gosh i maid up my mind if father licked me that i woodent ball and i wood do something auful the next day, i wont say what it was but it was something auful. i have been a prety mean feller.

Mar. 11, 186- when i got up this morning i felt buly, and i got a pail of water and brogt in wood enuf to fill the woodbox way over the top. it is warm and the snow is all gone xcept in the corners where the drifts were. i saw a robin today and i wished on it but i cant tell what i wished becaus if i did it woodent come true. it is something i have been wanting auful for a long time, but i havent had money enuf to buy it.

Mar. 12. rany. i went to church. the minister said it was esy to be good if you tride. i gess ministers dont know much ennyway.

Mar. 13. me and Beany is going to keep store in my shed. today we made the counter of 2 barils and a board and we made a lot of flyboxes and jacobs laders and tonite we made a lot of sweet firn cigars, and hayseed and mulen leaf and cornsilk. this afternoon we went out picking up bones in a baskit. most every yard had a lot of bones in it xcept where the fellers had been. we got most a buchel. we get half a cent a pound for them down to old Gechels store they make nife handels of them and perl buttons.

Mar. 14. Beany got mad today and says he wont keep store with me. we got our flyboxes all pined up and our boxes of cigars all ready and mother said she wood give me some molases for sweatened water. so we was all ready when Beany got mad about the sine. he wanted it to be Watson and Shute becaus he is older then me, but it was my shed and my sweatened water and my board and my barils and so i said my name shood come ferst and he got mad and took half of the things and went home. i dident let him have a bit of the sweatened water. Lucy Watson was mad two and woodent speek to Keene and Cele.

Mar. 15, 186- i opened my store today and nailed up my sine fancy goods and sweatened water H. Shute. Potter and Whack and Fatty and Boog and Puzzy and all the fellers come round and i sold lots of stuff. i charge 10 nails for a sweet firn cigar, 5 nails for a rattan or grape vine cigar and 3 nails for hayseed cornsilk and mullen leaf. 3 nails for white jacobs ladders and 5 for gilt, 10 nails for flyboxes made of writing book paper, and 15 and 20 nails for gilt and silver and red paper. 15 nails for snappers that will snap good, and 15 nails for a glass of sweatened water. i had a big trade and i cood see Beany out in frunt of his house looking over. bimeby he came over and i said hullo Beany come and have a drink and a cigar. so Beany he took a glass and drunk it and lit a cigar, a sweet firn one and said how is trade, and i said they is quite a little stiring, and he said have you got mutch stock and i said most sold out but they is plenty more where that come from and Beany he said dont you want to by my stuff and i said no i gess not. bimeby Beany he said less make up Plupy and i said i aint mad and Beany he said well let the old sine rip and so he went over and got his stuff and pinned it up and we had a good trade all the afternoon. tonite we made cigars and flyboxes and snappers. Beany is a prety good feller to have a store with only he smokes and drinks two mutch.

Mar. 16. Brite and fair. i saw a blewbird today. Beany come over erly and we had a good trade. Beany smoked so many sweet firn cigars and drank so mutch sweatened water that i told him he coodent be my pardner unless he smoked cheeper cigars and only drank 4 glasses a day. 2 in the morning and 2 in the evening. that is enuf for enny man.

Mar. 17. Rany today. not mutch trade. Pewt and Nipper has got a store in Pewts shed. Tomtit says he has got beter things than we have and he got all the fellers to go up there. Tomtit was mad becaus we woodent take sheet iron for pay. you cant get ennything for sheet iron down to old Getchels and if we took it for pay enny feller cood go out and pick up a old stove pipe and buy out your store.

Mar. 18. brite and fair. no i mean it is clowdy. Beany is acting prety queer. he has been talking with Pewt, and last nite he promised to come over and make cigars and he dident come and Nipper said Beany was over to Pewts. today he was prety sassy and said he would drink all the sweatened water he wanted. he was away all the afternoon.

Mar. 19. Beany dident make up enny faces behind the organ today. after church i holered at him and he woodent look round. i bet he is going to keep store with Pewt. i dont care.

Mar. 20. Beany came over this morning and said he was going to be pardner with Pewt and he wanted his stuff and his half of the iron and nails. I told him he was a mean cuss and he said he woodent be pardner with a feller whitch woodent let him drink and smoke out of the store. he said Pewt wasent so mean as all that. so we divided the stuff and Beany wanted half of what nails and iron i had taken before we were pardners. he dident get it you bet, and he dident get enny sweatened water neether.

Mar. 21. brite and fair. Medo Thirsten came up today and wanted to buy my stuff and i sold it all to him. i am glad to get out of the store so i can go of with Potter and Chick Chickering. we went up to the Eddy today. we saw some blackbirds and some robins and 3 blewbirds, and got 2 last years nests. it is almost time for flying squerels. we saw a redder today.

Mar. 22. I saw Beany today and he run out his tung at me. all rite for you Beany.

Mar. 23. it raned and was auful windy today. i sold my iron and bones today to old Getchel for 42 cents. i took out 12 cents to treet the fellers and put 30 cents with my cornet money.

Mar. 24. it was warm today and fine. I saw some wild geese flying over today. it made me feel funny to hear them holler. me and Potter and Chick went out in the woods today with our bows and arrows and bilt a fire and fride some potatose.

Mar. 25. this is the last day of vacation. Beany and Pewt have had a auful row, Beany says Pewt sold all the iron and nails and kept most of the money. Pewt says Beany drank up more then the moneys wirth of sweatened water and smoked all the best cigars i am glad of it. i gess the next time Beany will know more.

Mar. 26. sunday. nothing to do but go to church and think of going to school tomorow. i wonder if i shall get a licking this tirm.

Mar. 27. i went to school today. they isent much fun now. it is two muddy to play ennything. so the fellers all have clappers and we clap all the time. Skinny Bruce is the best one. he has some bone clappers that jest ring. Fatty Gilman has got some made of black walnut.

Mar. 28. we plaid ball a little today. it is geting prety dry in the school yard now.

Mar. 29. it snowed a little today and then melted. they wasent enuf for snow balling. my hens has begun to lay.

Mar. 30. the top of my roosters comb whitch was frose last winter when i was sick has come of and his comb is all smooth and shiny and hasent got enny picks on it.

Mar. 31. brite and fair tomorow is april fool day. i am going to get one on Beany.

Apr. 1. today i had a good one to get on Beany. i rung the doorbell of our house and mother came to the door and i stood there laffin and she laffed and said i am glad to see you sir because i want you to fill the woodbox and get me 5 pails of water. gosh i dident think it was so funny. at school old Francis woodent let us play april fools on each other but in the afternoon i went over to get Beany to come with me to get a 4 foot yardstick down to Lyfords. i was going to get Beany to ask for it and then they wood lam him, becaus they isent enny 4 foot yardstick. i jest laffed to think of Beany getting licked. well when i asked Beany he said he wood go only his father wanted him to go down to old Kellogs harness shop to get a pint of strap oil to oil some harnes, and if i wood go with him ferst he would go with me. so i said yes and we went. jest before we got there Beany said you go in and ask for it, and i will wait becaus old Kellog dont like me very well. so i went in and old Kellog was sitting straddle of a seet with big wooden nippers on it and he was sowing on a harness and he said cross like what do you want and i said i want a pint of strap oil and he said o yes i have got some good strap oil and he got down and grabed me by the coller and took down a strap and licked me till i hollered. then he let me go and when i went out rubing my legs Beany was jest laffing fit to die and he said you thought you was prety smart old Plupy to get me to go down for a 4 foot yard stick dident you. and then he ran his tung out and run of down town. i will pay Beany for that.

Apr. 2. brite and fair. i went to church.

Apr. 3. Father is going to have a garden and i have got to dig it up. Father says he is going to help me but i know how it will be. he will dig about ten minits and then he will go over to see Beanys father. i dont see why it is that jest as soon as it is time for fishing father wants to make me wirk. Pewt cought 3 pirch today.

Apr. 4. Brite and fair. last nite we went diging up the garden. father began to dig and dug about a minit and then he stoped and went in the house to change his shues, and then he come out and took of his coat and then he dug a nother minit and then he went to the fence and talked with Sam Dire and then he took of his vest and took up his spade and then he said i was doing splendid and he wanted to see Wats a minit and he went over to see Beanys father jest as i said he wood and dident come back. well i dug until mother called me in to go to bed and i got about a pan full of wirms. tonite me and father are going to dig some more. my back is lame.

Apr. 5. Brite and fair. last nite father told me to cut the eyes out of a lot of potatose to plant. so this noon and after school me and Keene and Cele cut out the eyes of the potatose. we raced to see which wood beet, i had a sharp spoon handel, Keene a darning needle, and Cele a pen-nife. we had 3 cups to put the eyes in and when we got the eyes all dug out we counted the eyes. Cele had 176 Keene 158 and i had 143. jest as we got done father came home, so we showed him the eyes and i wish you cood see him. i woodent dare to wright what he said. if i talked like he did he wood have sent me to bed for a year. i gess he wood have licked us all but mother laffed and laffed and said we dident know enuf about farming. so we only got sent to bed.

Apr. 6. brite and fair. i hoped it wood rane today so we coodent dig. but it dident. if they had been a circus it wood have raned like time. last nite we dug some more. father started all rite but jest then he said he had got to go down town with mother. so i dug until Beany and Pewt came over and then we begun to plug peaces of dirt at Charly Dire and after a while somebody broke a window in Sam Dires house. Pewt said it was me and Beany said it was Pewt. father came home and sent me to bed. he give Sam Dire 25 cents for the window. ennyway Pewt broke it.

Apr. 7. brite and fair.

Apr. 8, 186- it raned today. i am glad of it.

Apr. 9. it raned today. i am glad of it. i went to church.

Apr. 10. tonite me and Beany and Whack finished diging all the rest of the garden. when father came home he went out and steped on a rake that was lying down with the sharp points up and ran it into his foot and he came limping into the house swaring auful, but he wasent much hurt and isent going to have enny garden. ennyway he left the rake there himself.

Apr. 11, 186- Brite and fair. father is going to have some geese. he went to Dal Gilmors and Dal said you cood keep geese for nothing becaus all they et was grass and father says he can raise geese on grass until October and then kill them and sell them and make lots of money. ennyway they was grass enuf becaus we want going to have enny garden since father steped on the rake. Dal Gilmor has got a old goose whitch is more then 30 years old. i bet he is tuf.

Apr. 12. Brite and fair. father came home tonite erly and we begun to make a geese pond. we took a baril and cut it in 2 and made 2 tubs. then we dug a hole in the garden and put in 1 tub and filled it with water. it made a buly pond. next saterday father is coming home erly and we are going to hampton falls to get sum geese eggs.

Apr. 13. Rany Franky fell out of bed last nite. father said it was my falt. the baby had the crupe. father says something is always the matter.

Apr. 14. clowdy but no rane. beany has got a dog, it is black and tan, not 2 dogs but jest 1. his name is Gip and he can fite.

Apr. 15. still clowdy. Frank Hanes has got a dog like Beanys. his name is Dime, i bet he can fite.

Apr. 16. brite and fair. i put some minnies in the geese pond today. it was after church and i got them yesterday. they wood have dide in the tin pail, so it wasent rong to put them in Sunday. tomorow we are going down to get the geese eggs.

Apr. 17. brite and fair. i am wrighting this in bed. it has been a prety tuf day i tell you. father coodent come home erly becaus he had to wirk, so he give me fifty cents and me and Beany went down to hampton falls after the geese eggs. well we got them and started home. we had Beanys fathers horse and we saw a old black horse by the side of the road and Beany said i wood like to plug him with a geese egg, i said praps they is a roten egg there. so we shook the eggs till by and by they was one whitch ratled. then Beany choze to plug him and he let ding at him and the egg hit him a paister rite in the side and broak and spatered him all over with yellow, and he kicked up and ran away before i cood get a nother egg. then we went on till we saw 2 cows and we shook the eggs again till we got 2 whitch ratled and when we went by we stood up in the wagon and let ding at the cows. i hit one rite in the frunt of her head and the yellow ran down over her nose and Beany hit the other in the side and then a man holered at us and we licked the horse and drove of lively. then we saw a cat sitting in a barn door and we both let ding at her but dident hit her and both eggs smached agenst the barn and the cat ran into the barn and a man came out with a tin pail in his hand and a little stool in the other and holered at us and we licked up the horse again. after that we dident plug enny more for they was only 7 eggs left and they only ratled a little. when we got home Beany let me out and i told father about the eggs being roten, he was prety mad and said i had aught to have shook them before i took them. he asked me what i did with the roten eggs and i said i threw them away and jest then Mister Watson Beanys father came over with Beany and 2 men and it was the same man whose horse we pluged with roten eggs, and the man who holered at us when we plugged the old cows. the man grabed me by the coller and told father i was the wirst boy in the town and if father dident lick me out of my skin he wood, and father said hold on there, they aint nobody going to lick my boy unless he licks me ferst, and he walked up to the man prety quick, and the man let go my coller and father said if they is any licking to be done i can do all that is necesary, and the man said we are going to have him arested, and father said what has he done and the man said these two boys have been throwing rocks at my horse and have cut a big gash in his side and he is all over blud, and the other man said we had been pluging rocks at his cows and had cut one on the head and one on the side well me and Beany said we only threw geese eggs at them and the blud was the runny part of the eggs and we crossed our throtes and hoped to die if it wasent so, and father said to the man did you xamine the gash and he said he was so mad when he see the horse that he hitched up the other horse and followed us and told his hired man to look after the horse and brogt the other man to. so father said to Beanys father to hich up his horse and we wood go down and see if we had lied to him and he said if i had lied to him he wood give me the wirst licking i ever had. well jest as we were going to get in the wagon the man whitch had the tin pail and the stool in his hand come driving up and said we had been pluging roten eggs at his barn and father said he wood be cussed if he ever saw such boys, and me and Beany said we dident mean to hit the barn but we pluged at the cat and dident hit her. then the other men told him about the horse and cows and he said it was only roten eggs and then they felt beter, and they said they was willing to let us of with a good licking, but father said he woodent lick me for ennybody else, but he wood pay them for their truble and they said they wood settle for fifty cents each and i had to pay it out of my cornet money. i only had one dollar and 30 cents but Aunt Sarah give me 20 cents. i beleive i had rather got a licking for it will take me 6 weaks to ern so much money and i wood have got over a licking as soon as i got to sleep. then father sent me to bed. i wonder if Beanys father licked him. i shall know tomorow.

Apr. 18. Brite and fair. Beany dident get licked.

Apr. 19. Brite and fair. i bet father cood have licked those 3 hampton falls men together easy.

Apr. 20. Brite and fair. i shall never get that cornet.

Apr. 21. i had some fun today. they wasent enny school today becaus old Francis had to go to a funeral or something. so i bilt a nest for my hens.

Apr. 22. Brite and fair. father aint going to have enny geese. tonite we got a old yellow hen of Sam Dire and set her on 7 eggs in the horse-stal, and then we had super. nothing hapened at super xcept that Keene got sent to bed for sticking out her tung at father when she thought he wasent looking but he was, becaus he woodent let her go over to see Lucy Watson Beanys sisters new hat. well after it was dark father said i forgot to pay Sam for his hen and he started rite acros the garden to go over to Sam Diars and it was dark and i herd a auful splash and thumping round and feerful swaring and i knew father was in the geese pond. i woodent dass to wright down what he said, if i had said what he did he wood have sent me to bed for a year. well he came limping home and swaring into the house and he made me get a lanten and we went out to the barn and he took the old hen by her hind legs and swung her round jest as we fellers do when we plug apples on a stick and pluged her way over in Sam Diars yard and then he took the eggs and pluged them as far as he cood and told me to fill up the pond tomorow or he wood lick me. then we went in and mother and aunt Sarah nearly killed themselves laffin and father said i spose you wood laff if i killed myself and when i went up to bed i laffed easy and Keene and Cele were laffing under the bed close. bimeby i herd father laffin and then we all laffed loud. jest think i had to pay a dollar and a half of my cornet money for pluging 5 eggs and father pluged 7 eggs and a old hen and dident have to pay ennything, ennyway it was fun to see him.

Apr. 23. Brite and fair. i filled up the geese pond. it was sunday but it was after dark.

Apr. 24. Brite and fair. when father came home i told him i had filled up the geese pond and he asked me where the tub was and when i said i had filled it up he said i was a loonatic and dident know enuf to go in when it raned. so he made me dig out the tub and fill in the hole. i tell you i have to wirk prety hard.

Apr. 25. Brite and fair. today old man Thirsten Medos father came to the house and told mother someone had pluged roten eggs at his barn. mother dident know what to say for a minit for she dident want to tell about fathers falling into the geese pond, so she said she was very sure i hadent done it but she wood speak to father about it, so when father got home old man Thirsten came up to the house and said George that cussid boy of yours has been pluging roten eggs at my barn and father said this time Kimball, his name is Kimball, he dident do it for he was with me all the evening til he went to bed. so father and old man Thirsten went down to see the barn and it was all spatered with yellow. then old man Thirsten said he wood give a dolar to know who the scowndril was whitch pluged those eggs, and father said i wish you cood Kimball, it is a outrage, and father looked auful funny, jest as he did when he scart old Ike Shute that time on the high school steps. when we went home father kept laffing, and when he told mother she said it was a shame and he aught to make it rite with him, and so father bought a sawhoss of him, he sells sawhosses, and i have got to use it. somehow i always get the wirst of it.

Apr. 26, 186- it raned like time last nite but it was brite and fair when i got up. what do you think, me and Beany are going to by a horse of old Nat Mason. he lives down Stratam road and he has a old troter that can go like time.

Apr. 27. brite and fair. me and Beany saw old Nat today. we aint got enny chink. if i hadent paid that money to those hampton falls men for pluging roten eggs at there cows i should have sum. all i can rase is thirty five cents and Beany can rase fifteen cents. Fatty Gilman most always has lots of chink.

Apr. 28. me and Beany saw Fatty today. he wants to go in with us becaus he says his folks want to use old Chub so mutch that he dont get enny chance to use him. but Fatty he hasent got enny chink eether. enny way we are going to see old Nat tomorrow and peraps he will let us have it on tick.

Apr. 29. brite and fair. today was saterday and this afternoon me and Beany and Fatty went down to see old Nat. he was in a old house smoking a old pipe made out of a corn cob. so Fatty he asked him to show us his old plug, only Fatty dident say old plug but said Mister Mason can we see your troting horse, and old Nat he got up and went to a little barn and opened the door and holered get up lady Clara and she tride to get up and coodent, and old Nat swoar and kicked her and then she coodent get up, and then he clim over her and puled her head up into the rack and then he took a stick and hit her sum more and swoar sum more and then she got up. then Beany he asked old Nat what made her not get up and he said that troting horses most never laid down more than once or twict a weak and sum of the best troters never laid down. he said Dexter and Flora Tempel never was knowed to lay down. then Fatty asked him to let us see her trot and he hiched her into a buggy and we set on the fence and old Nat he drove of most walking. bimeby we herd the old wagon ratling and old Nat he came down the street just fluking. I never saw a horse go so fast. i tell you old Nat he had to pull to stop her. she breethed prety hard and jerky, but Nat he said it was hickups becaus she had et too mutch. Fatty he asked how old she was and old Nat he said she was bout 12 but that she wood be good til she was 30. Then we asked how mutch he wood sell her for and he said he wanted 5 dolers for her but he wood let us have her for 2 dolars and fifty cents and we could have the wagon for 2 dolars and fifty cents two, and he wood throw in the harnes. but we dident have the money and so we tride to swap and bimeby he said if i wood give him my gun and Fatty wood give him his silver pensil case and Beany give him his 6 bladed nife he wood trust us for a month. so we give him the things and he give us the horse. only we coodent take her then becaus we have got to find a place to keep her. none of us dass to tell our folks about it. we woodent let Fatty know about it if we hadent suposed he had plenty of chink.

Apr. 30. brite and fair. after church today we went round to see if we cood get a place to keep our horse. we asked

Noot Crumet but Noot he said he dident have enny place to put her unles he give her his room and he told us to go to Bucher Haly and see if we coodent get a chanse to put her in his smoke house for we cood keep her longer there than enny where else and so we went to him and he chased us out of his yard. then we went to Charles Flanders but he dident have but one room and his shed wasent big enuf to keep a gote, and then we went over to old Jethrow Simpsons and Jethrow he said if we wood help him haul wood enuf to fill his shed we cood keep her in his barn as long as we wanted to and have enuf hay two.

May 1. it was may day today and we dident have enny school. so me and Beany went up to Fattys and got him and we went down to old Nats. We wood have run all the way only Fatty got tukered out. When we got there old Nat made us promise to give him a hat or a pair of old boots becaus he kept lady Clara over Sunday. Fatty he said they was lots of old hats at home and so we went way back and got a old tall bever hat and then old Nat hiched up lady Clara and we piled in. Fatty he drove ferst becaus he said we coodent have got her unless he had got the old tall bever. so Fatty he drove up as fur as ass brook and then Beany he drove as fur as the old brick meeting house and then i drove as fur as the hall place where Jethrow lives. we all had to stand up when we drove becaus the ranes is two short. when we got there old Jethrow was there and he had a dingel cart and we hiched lady Clara into it and went up to Jady Hill for sum wood. we wirked till 12 oh clock and then we run home to dinner and run back agen. i took all the meal i had for my hens most 2 quarts and i fed her. it is Fattys tirn next to get meal for her. then we wirked til six oh clock and we were allmost ded we were so tired. well when we asked old Jethrow whitch stal we shood put her in he told us to take our old plug and get out or he wood lick us. jest think of that. well we dident know what to do. so we waited til most dark and then Beany said we had beter go to the next house becaus they was a big shed there. so i said i wood ring if Fatty wood ask and so i rung the bell and a woman came to the door and Fatty told her all about it and she said old Jethrow was a meen old skin flint and we cood put our horse in her shed and cood keep her their as long as we wanted to. so she give us a lantern and we went out and they was a buly place and we made a stal with 2 boards and put a lot of saw dust under her and give her a pale of water only we dident have enny hay. well bimeby Beany said that he cood see the hay sticking out of the cracks in old Jethrows barn, and we went over and looked and we cood see plenty of hay there. so Fatty he said we had ernt that hay and we aught to have it, and Beany said so two, and Fatty said he woodent steal ennything but this hay was ours and we had ernt it. so Fatty and Beany puled out a board and held it open while i puled out enuf hay and then we fed lady Clara and went home. ennyway the hay was ours and it wasent stealing to take it.

May 2. brite and fair. this morning i got up erly and went over to the barn. Beany he was there and Fatty he came after i had got there. lady Clara was laying down and woodent get up. i gess she was prety tired. so we fed her and Fatty brogt some otes. so we curred her down as far as we cood reech and brushed her and then we went home. at brekfast mother asked me what made me smel so barny and i said i had been helping Fatty curry his horse. at noon we fed her agen and tonite we got her up and curred her other side. we dident drive her today.

May 3. rany as time. we cant drive lady Clara today. we curred her 2 times.

May 4. tonite we drove lady Clara. We went down Newmarket road. we took tirns driving. one of the wheals come of and we had to get out and walk home holding on the wheal.

May 5. Ed Adams give us a nut and we fixed the wheal. we had a ride tonite. i tell you lady Clara can go. we beat Gim Lovering tonite. he dident know who we was becaus it was two dark but we knowed him. we beat him and then we waited for him to come up and then we beat him agen. we did that 3 times, and Gim he was mad.

May 6. my hens dont lay enny now. i gess i dont give them enuf to eat. it is prety hard to keep a horse and hens two. we dident drive tonite becaus it raned. it was brite and fair yesterday.

May 7. today was sunday and we coodent drive lady Clara. tomorrow nite we are going to lay for old man Churchil with his troter. i bet we can beat him.

May 8. i have missed in my lesons most every day, and so has Fatty and Beany. today i swaped a hen for a buchel of meal for lady Clara. we drove her tonite but we dident find ennyone to race.

May 9. brite and fair. if Beany dont shell out more meal he wont drive lady Clara agen.

May 10. Beany got a peck of meal today at old Si Smiths. he charged it to his father.

May 11. we had a buly ride tonite we raced 4 fellers and beat them.

May 12. brite and fair. tonite we coodent get lady Clara up. we are going to try agen tomorrow and drive her in the day time.

May 13. rany agen. we got lady Clara up this morning. Beany and Fatty pulled in front and i licked behind. this afternoon one of our wheals broak down. Ed Adams give us a nother wheal. it went on all rite only it isent as big as the other wheals and it makes the wagon go one sided a little. we had a good ride today. we have to be pretty careful in tirning around a corner becaus the wagon is one sided.

May 14. today was sunday. father told me if i smelt so of the barn he woodent let me go up to Fattys agen. i bet he wood be mad if he knowed i oned a horse.

May 15. there was a fite in school today. i dont care mutch about fites now. i had ruther race horses. tonite we raced with a big white horse and beat him esy. we all had to pull on the ranes to stop lady Clara.

May 16. brite and fair. Beany is behind 5 feeds and me and Fatty had to make it up. last nite lady Clara lost a shue. so this morning before school we walked every where we drove last nite and Beany found the shue way down to long meter Dows on Hamton road. Beany he said if we wood call it square about the feeds he wood get Gim Elerson to nale on the shue. so we did and Beany got Gim to nale on the shue. Beany he raked up Gims front yard to pay him. Beany is a prety good feller. Fatty had company to his house and we dident go to ride tonite. it was two bad.

May 17. rany as time. we coodent go to ride today. it always ranes jest when a feller wants to do some thing.

May 18. it raned all yesterday and last nite and today. i bet it will rane a week. we are having prety tuf luck.

May 19. at last it has stoped raning. i thaught i never shood wright brite and fair agen. we had a buly ride tonite after we had tide up the bridle with sum rope. lady Clara fell down and we had to unharnes her and get her up. she broak the bridle and skined her gnees and we put on sum wheal greese. Beany was standing up driving when she fell down and it draged him rite over the dasher and on top of lady Clara. tomorow they is going to be a ministers meeting in the upper church and there aint enny school tomorow. so we are going to drive all day. after school we washed the harness and got a load of sawdust at the hub mill, and curred lady Clara. we have got most all the hay we can reech. when we cant reech enny more i dont know where we can get enny more unless Fatty can get sum.

May 21. Brite and fair. i had a feerful day yesterday. i feel so bad i cant hardly wright ennything. but i will try to wright it all down. in the morning me and Beany and Fatty we hiched up lady Clara and drove round town. sum of the fellers holered at us but we dident care. they was lots of ministers in town. they was mostly long tailers with white necktis. so in the afternoon we hiched up agen and drove up to the depot. old woodbridge Odlin was there wating for the 2 oh clock trane. he had a baruch with a driver and his new span of black horses with cliped tails. and he had on his long tailed black coat and a shiny bever hat. well we dident wate for the trane but we drove through Winter street and out to Front street. when we came to Lincoln street old Woodbridge Odlin came along with his baruch filled with old ministers with bever hats and specks and white necktis, and the driver hit the horses and away they went lickity larup. well Beany he was driving and he leened over and hit lady Clara a paist with the whip and she went after them like chane litening, and we all began to yell and the black horses went faster. well they was 2 rods ahead and when we got to Whackers house we was most up to there hind wheel, and when we got to doctor Gorams office we was jest even. the old ministers was bouncing around and holding on to the sides, and old Woodbridge had lost his hat and was standing up yelling sumthing at the driver, and his whiskers were blowing way behind him. it makes me most die to think of him but i dont feel mutch like laffin. well when we got to Elliott street we were ahead of them and then the driver began to pull up his horses becaus all the people was yelling and waving there hats like time. well lady Clara was breething so she sounded like a big sawmill saw, and when we tride to stop her she woodent stop so we all tride together but we coodent pull her in a mite she had her tail sticking rite up in the air and the more we pulled the faster she went, when we went thru the square Fatty holered to run her over string brige and up factory hill so we cood stop her, and we pulled as hard as we cood but when she came to the corner she tirned around into Water street and over went the wagon and we came out jest fluking. well we want hurt mutch and we run after her as fast as we cood. we found pieces of the wagon and harnes all over the street and when we got to the barn she was there all rite. lots of people came to see about it, but when they found that nobody was hurt they went away. they wasent ennything of the harnes left but the bridle and the wagon was everywhere along the street. Well when father came home somebody had told him about it and he made me tell him all about it, where we got her and how we fed her and everything, and when i told him about the hay i thought he was going to lick time out of me he was so mad, and he said he never knowed i cood steal, and i said i only hooked it and he said what is the diference and i said stealing is taking sumthing that you know belongs to sumbody else, and hooking is taking sumthing that belongs to you and sumbody else wont let you have. i suposed everybody knowed that. well he dident lick me, but after super he got mister Watson, Beanys father and we all went over to see lady Clara and what do you think, when we got there she was ded. i gess she had broak something inside of her. i tell you me and Beany felt prety bad and Fatty did when we told him. well then father and mister Watson Beanys father told us to go home and go to bed and so we went. so tonite i herd father telling mother about it and he said he give old Jethrow a dresing down that wood tech him not to cheet a boy agen. he said if Jethrow hadent been a old man he wood have nocked his head of.

May 22. brite and fair. i shal never own a horse agen.

May 23, 186- brite and fair. my hens are laying buly now. i gess they dident have very good cair when me and Beany and Fatty was keeping Lady Clara. i tell you a feller witch keeps a horse cant pay mutch atention to ennything else.

May 24. brite and fair. tonite me and father went down to old man Collins. he wants to sell father his cow. he says she gives 20 quats of milk a day. father says the milk we get of the milk man is all chork and water.

May 25. rany as time. father ofered 30 dolars for old man Collins cow. he wants 35 dolars. she has got auful long horns. old man Collins said she had auful big milk vanes. father said they was varrycose vanes and she want wirth 30 dolars but he wood give it to help out a old man. old man Collins he said if she kep on giving milk the way she was a giving it they wood have to milk her in a tub. then father he said he gessed she give so mutch milk that it want good for ennything and old man Collins he said you cood take the creem up by one corner and lift it out like a old pair of linen britches. they dident trade tonite.

May 26. brite and fair. tonite me and father went down to old man Collins agen. father said he was going to trade for that cow only i must shet up and not say ennything. he said you jest wach me and you will lern sumthing about trading. so i wached him. well we went down and father said well mister Collins how do you feel about trading tonite. and old man Collins he said, i gess you are two late George fer i have sold her to a man in Hamton Falls. and father said what did you get for her and old man Collins he said i told him he cood have her for 35 dolars and he ofered me 33 dolars and 50 cents and i said the first man whitch ofers me 35 dolars gets her, and i gess he will be up tomorow morning. then father he said have you made the trade and old man Collins he said he hadent made enny trade but he had kind of let the man understand he cood have her for 35 dolars. then father he said he wood give 35 dolars and old man Collins he said he dident know about selling her xcept to the Hamton Falls man but if father wood give him 37 dolars he cood give the Hamton Falls man 2 dolars if he came up and was disapointed. so father he give old man Collins 37 dolars and we got a roap and tide it round her horns and led her home. when we got home we tried to get her in the barn, father he went ahead and she folowed him in and all of a suddin she backed out lively and father came out jest fluking, holding on to the roap and taking feerful long stradles. he looked so mad that i dident dass to laff. well father held on like a good feller and bimeby she stoped. then father said so so and held out sum meal in a pail and got her in the barn and tide her to a post. then he give her sum hay and we went in and he told mother she had beter make sum araingments to sell sum milk for we was going to have 20 quats every day. then mother she said if the cow gives milk like my hens lade egs they woodent be mutch milk to sell, and father said you jest wait til morning. then we went down to old Gechels store and father he bougt the bigest milk pail he cood find.

May 27. brite and fair. this morning me and father got up erly and we went out to feed the cow and i piched down the hay and father he set down and begun to milk her, he brougt out the big pail and a little one to use after he had filled the big one. well the ferst thing he did was to aim a streem rite in my eye. then he milked in the pail and it made a funy sound, well he kep milking and bimeby it stoped coming, and he squeazed away as hard as he cood and he coodent get a drop and bimeby he give up and said he gessed it was becaus she was in a new place and was loansum. when we went into the house and straned it thrugh a siv they wasent quite 2 quats. mother she laffed and asked what he had done with the other 8 quats and father he said you wait til tonite. then he et his brekfast and went to boston and i et mine and drove the old cow to pasture. i found a robins nest in a pine tree and took one eg. it is all rite to take one becaus the old bird cant count.

May 28, 186- brite and fair. last nite after super father milked the old cow again. he only got 2 quats and a half. he was prety mad and he said he wood get even with old man Collins sum day. tonite he met old man Collins and he asked father if she milked esy and father said yes and he asked father how mutch she give and father said she give more than he wanted. that want a lie for father dont like milk. i bet father will get even with him sum day. nothing else today but church.

May 29. brite and fair. i have to go to pasture 2 times every day. i like to go in the woods but i dont like to have to go. today i found a nest in the barn with 15 hens egs. i gess mother wont say mutch about my hens now.

May 30. Rany. Beany has gone to Bideford to see Tom Cleves. i hope Tom will come with him when Beany comes home. i went up to Whacker Chadwicks tonite. Beany has been sick he et two mutch pork.

May 31. today it was hot and we had a thunder shower. it raned when i was driving the old cow from pasture and i made her run from old Nat Gordons way home. Sam Dire said she wood give bludy milk, so when father milked her i wached and it want a bit red. so i gess she is all rite.

June 1. brite and fair. today we had a great time at brekfast. father was home becaus sumtimes he gets tired. we had boiled egs for brekfast and mother she boiled the egs i found in the nest. well we set down to the table and father he helped us to egs and bisket and he took up a eg and held it over his glass and hit it a paist with his spoon and it went off jest like a pop pistol and father he said thunder Joey the infernal thing is roten and we all held our nose and ran away from the table and you never smelt such a auful smel. well mother she made me take the egs all out behine the barn and throw them away and i did and when i got there i had sum fun pluging them at J. Albert Clarks big apple tree and i hit it most every time and every time i hit it the eg popped like a pistol. then i went in to brekfast and mother was burning some coffy in a duspan to take away the smel of the roten eg. well while we was eating brekfast J. Albert Clark he came in and said i had beter come out and clean of his apple tree and burn a rag and father made me take a pail of hot water and clean it of. J. Albert needent have been so fusy for it wood have all dride in a little while.

June 2. brite and fair. i wish that old cow was ded. Beany hasent got back yet.

June 3. brite and fair. i am in bed. i aint sick only i havent got enny close to wair. tonite after father had milked the old cow i thougt i wood try it. so i got a tin diper and went out and set down and began to squeaze and she kicked me rite thrugh the barn door and rite into the manure pile. when i got up i was all covered and Aunt Clark was in her back garden and she saw me and asked me if i was hurt and i said i wasent and she said for mersy sakes dont come near me but go round to the pump. well i went round to the pump and mother and Aunt Sarah and Aunt Clark pumped on me and threw pails of water on me and scraped me with peaces of shingle, and when they had got me prety clean mother made me go in the barn and take of my close and then she put me in a tub in the kichen and washed me in warm water and soped my head and then sent me to bed. i have got to wair my best close tomorow and i cant go out of the yard. i wish that old cow was ded. father said it sirved me jest rite.

June 4. Brite and fair. Beany has got back. tonite he came over and told me about the fun he had at Bideford. we was going to ring doorbells tonite but i had to stay in the yard and it was sunday two.

June 5. Brite and fair. today Scotty Brigam let me take his bugle and i lerned to make 2 notes. my mouth was all sweled up and my face aked. it aint so esy as a tin whissle but i can make more noise on it. i gess i shall never get that cornet.

June 6, 186- i have to pay all the money i can ern to get corn for my hens.

June 7. Brite and fair in the morning and clowdy but no rane in the afternoon. tonite me and Beany rung doorbells. we dident get cougt but we came prety near it.

June 8. Rany. Tonite the old cow kicked father and nocked him rite of the stool and spilt about a quat of milk all over him. buly. i wanted to tell him it sirved him rite but i dident dass to.

June 9. Clowdy but no rane. father has sold the old cow to Eben Garland the bucher. buly. Aunt Sarah asked mother what she gessed he wood have next and mother she said she gessed he wood by a gristly bear for he had bougt most everything but that. he says he gesses he will have sum sheap for they cant bite or kick and dont eat mutch.

June 10. brite and fair. the baby had the croop last nite. the minit he coffed croopy father and mother jumped out of bed and father he fell over a chair and that waked us all up. then he tride to lite a lamp and he coodent find the maches and he swoar round feerful. well mother she lit the lamp and they all went tearing round and they got sum hot water and made the baby eat some eg and sugar and put hot close on his neck and prety soon he was all rite. then they give me the rest of the eg and sugar. then we all went to bed and i lay and laffed to think of father tumbling over the chair and swaring. Ennyway the baby is all rite.

June 11. i hate to go to church. we have all got to be vaxinated. sum peeple in the next town have got the small pocks. Beany has been and Pewt two. Beany says the doctor takes a nife and cuts a hole in your arm and then puts on a big scab whitch has come of somebodys arm whitch has been vaxinated, and that stops the blud. but he says that if the scab dont fit you bleed to deth. so i asked father about it tonite and he said that Beany lied about it, but he says if you are vaxinated with the scab of a redheaded person your hair will turn red, and if he has warts or frekles you will have warts two and frekles. father said once when he was a boy he knew a feller whitch was vaxinated with a scab of a cock-eyed man and bimeby the feller began to squint and he kep on squinting wirse and wirse and bimeby he was cock-eyed two. and father he said he knew another feller whitch had a wooden leg and he sent his scab to another feller to be vaxinated and that feller began to limp and he always walked stifleged. i gess father was fooling.

ennyway i hope i shant be vaxinated with Skinny Bruces scab, becaus he is redheaded. father he said he was going to get a scab of Horis Cobb for me and perhaps i wood have a little fat on me and not be so spindel shanked. i wish i cood get a scab of Gim Erly or Tady Finton and i cood lick time out of Pewt.

June 12. brite and fair. Beany has a auful sore arm. he dont dass to rassle or fite or do ennything.

June 13. brite and fair. Pewt has got one two. tomorrow nite the doctor is coming.

June 15. brite and fair. last nite after super the doctor come and he went into the parlor and father and mother and Cele and Keene and me and Georgie and Annie and Frank and the baby was all in the setting room. well ferst father went in and he was only in there a few minits and he dident holler enny and then he come out laffing, and i asked him whose scab he had and he said he dident know but it must have been from sum minister becaus he had been thanking the lord it was all over. then mother she went in and father told her he had got the scab of old Mike Casey for her. mother is english and she dont like the irish and father said it to plage her. well she went in and then Aunt Sarah went in and Keene and Cele and they dident holler eether. then my tern came and i went in and it dident hurt a bit only sort of smarted tickly like. i asked the doctor whose scab i had and he said Bruce Brigams. buly. Bruce Brigam is the best cornet player in town. i bet i can play like time if i ever get a cornet. then the rest of them went in and none of them hollered xcept the baby and he always hollers when ennything is the matter. father told Cele that he got old Nigger Tashs scab for her and he gessed she wood begin to turn prety dark culored before a week or 2. Aunt Sarah told Cele he was fooling.

June 16, 186- Brite and fair. my arm is all rite.

June 17. Rany and thunderry. my arm begins to ich a little only i cant scrach it.

June 18. still rany. all our arms begin to ich. Annies arm is the wirst. we dident go to church today. That is one good thing. I never knew it to rane before on sunday.

June 19. brite and fair. every one of us is cross as time. i took hold of Georgies arm today and she began to ball and said i did it purpose. i keep hiting my arm agenst things all the time. somehow i never hit the well one. that is always the way with things.

June 20. brite and fair. father is cross two. last nite he grabed me by the arm to shake me and it hurt so i hollered like time, and then he let me go and said he forgot about my arm.

June 21. brite and fair. Annie is in bed sick with her arm. She always has things the wirst xcept mother, only mother says she hasent enny time to be sick.

June 22. brite and fair. my arm is still auful sore and the wirst of it is becaus i cant go in swimming.

June 23. Brite and fair. All our arms is better. John Johnson who rings the town bell has gone away for a week and Beanys father is going to ring it. He has to ring it at 7 oh clock in the morning and at 1 oh clock in the afternoon and at 9 oh clock in the nite except Saturday nites when they ring it at 8 oh clock so that peeple can get there baths before bedtime. Me and Beany are going to lern to ring it.

June 24. Rany. me and Beany went up to the church today to see Beanys father ring the town bell, he let us pull it a little, it is prety esy. then we went up at 1 oh clock and at 9 oh clock.

June 25. Rany again. most of our scabs has come of. i dident go up to see Mister Watson ring the bell this morning becaus i dident get up in time, it was sunday. Beany he dident neether, but we did tonite. Beany can ring it prety well.

June 26. Brite and fair. jest think, Beanys father is going to Portsmuth tomorrow and Beany is going to ring the bell and he is going to let me help him. Beany is a prety good feller. mother sent of the scabs today to peeple whitch wanted them. nobody wanted mine. father said it was becaus i was such a tuf feller.

June 27. Brite and fair. gosh if we dident have a auful time today. in the morning me and Beany went up to the church and rung the bell, we had a good time and rung it jest so many rings jest as mister Watson, Beanys father told us to, then me and Beany both got kep after school, and when we got out we asked Noot Crummet what time it was and he said it was jest 1 oh clock and that the town bell had jest struck and then me and Beany jest put for the church as tite as we cood hiper, and we was prety near tuckered out when we got there and we both grabed hold of the roap and begun to ring the bell. well we only rung it a few times before we herd sumone holler fire, and then more peeple begun to holler and we looked out and we saw Charles Fifield and Charly Batcheldor and Chick Randall and Jimmy Josie jest putting it for the ingine house, and Beany said buly they is a fire, and we begun to ring the bell as hard as we cood and holler fire. then the Methydist bell begun to ring and then the upper house bell, and Charles Tolls horses came galoping down to the fountain ingine house with Mat Sleeper driving. And Mager Blakes horses went by jest lickety larup for the Torrent ingine house with old Brown driving, and then Flunk Ham came piling into the church and said, give me that roap and he puled like time, then sum peeple came runing in and said where is the fire, and Flunk he said we dident know, and then we herd the ingine and went out and they was the Torrent and the fountain and lots of men, and they said where in hel is the fire and nobody knowed where it was. and then Chick Randall he asked Flunk what he was ringing the bell for and Flunk he said he found me and Beany ringing it. then they asked us what we was ringing it for and we said we was ringing it for Mister Watson Beanys father, because he was going to ring it for Mister Johnson, and he had to go to Portsmuth and so he told Beany to ring it, and then old Brown he said us was fools and asked us if we dident know enuf to tell time and he said it was only 20 minits past 12 oh clock when the bell begun to ring, and some of the peeple was mad and said we had aught to be arested, and then we said that Noot Crummet told us it was 1 oh clock and then sum of them begun to laff and said it was a good one. Ennyway me and Beany run home as quick as we cood and the peeple went of two. well tonite father said if he had got into so many scrapes when he was a boy as me and Beany did he wood have been in jale. and Aunt Sarah laffed and said she gessed she cood tell a few things if she wanted to and father he said he cood two but he gessed he woodent. Ennyway he said Gim Melcher and Charles Talor led him into a good many scrapes and Aunt Sarah she said she gessed me and Beany and Pewt want a sercumstance to father and Gim Melcher and Charles Talor.

June 28. brite and fair. it is most fourth of July again. they is going to be a band concert on the square. i shant have as mutch money as last year. ennyway i bet i will have a good time. i went in swiming 4 times today. i coodent go in while my arm was sore. Annie is most well but cross as time.

June 29. brite and fair. i went in swiming 5 times today. tomorow me and Pewt is going pikerilling. Pewt is a good feller to fish. fourth of July is coming next week.

June 30. today me and Pewt went fishing. We got Charles Flanders little blew bote. it is the esiest bote to row i ever rowd. Pewt cougt 4 pikeril and 5 kivies and 3 pirch. i cougt 2 pikeril and 2 kivies and 4 pirch and 1 sucker. we cougt sum minnies and shiners for bate but we dident call them ennything. we div of the bank at the eddy, once Pewt sliped and come down all guts, it nocked the wind all out of him.

July 1. brite and fair. today is the first day of July, and we had my fish fride for brekfast.

July 2. brite and fair. i bougt 5 bunches of snapcrackers and 2 bunches of canon crackers and sum slow mach and put them in a box in my room. tomorow is the nite before fourth. Pewt is going to have a pistol and Beany a canon. father he says if he hears of me fooling with a gun he will lick me and send me to bed for a week. ennyway he dident say ennything about a pistol or a canon.

July 3. gosh i was scart today. this morning i went up to my room to look at my snap crackers. i got the box on the floor and was counting them when i looked out of the window. i saw old Miss Hartnett hanging out sum close on the line, i thougt i cood make her gump and i wanted to try jest one canon cracker to see if they was good ones. well i lit one and pluged it down behind her, and jest as she was reaching up with her mouth full of close pins it went of bang, and she hollered love of God and went rite over backwards. i thougt i shood die and jest then one went of bang rite in the room and then they all begun to go of bang bang bang and i grabed the box up and pluged it out of the window and mother came up jest hipering and the room was full of smoke and i was stamping out the burning paper. well when i got it out she was prety mad with me and made me clean the room and wash the floor and windows. ferst i went out and picked up my snapcrackers. they were all rite but all the canon crackers but 2 had went of. Mother she asked me how they got afire and i said i was fooling with them and they got on fire and i had to plug them out of the window. then she said that was what fritened Miss Hartnett so and i said was she fritened and she said she was so fritened that she fell over backwards and i said is that so. mother dont know i did it on purpose whitch is prety good luck for me, so she only made me keep my snapcrackers in the yard. so i put them in a hole in the apple tree. gosh, you aught to hear Miss Hartnett tell about it.

July 7, 186- brite and fair. i have been in bed 3 days. on the fourth i got bloan up with Pewts canon. i had fired all my snapcrackers but 2 bunches whitch i had saved for nite, so me and Pewt we was fixing the canon, ferst we wood put in sum powder and then we wood put in sum wet paper for a wod and then we wood put in sum grass and then put in the ramrod and pound it down with a rock. then we wood put a fuze of a snap cracker in the tuch hole and lite it and put for the other side of the street and it wood make an auful bang and tern 2 or 3 sumersets. Well we had lots of fun and bimeby i was poaring out sum powder out of the powder horn and all of a suddin they was a flash of litening and the next i knew i was in bed and father and mother and Cele and Keene and docter Perry and aunt Sarah and aunt Clark and Georgie was in the room, and i said what is the matter and mother began to laff and then to cry and Docter Perry he said you had better take her out and let her lie down, but mother she said she wood be all rite and docter he said you needent wurry Missis Shute, you coodent kill this boy with brik. well my eyes smarted and i felt like the room was spinning round but it dident hurt enny. well that nite i coodent go to the band concert but they pushed my bed up to the window and i cood hear it prety good. the next day i had sum buly gelly and oranges and Cele and Keene read to me and in the afternoon Beany came in to see me. Beany he burnt his hand on the fourth and Pewt he burnt of one eyebrow and so we all had a prety good fourth. Yesterday Boog and Puzzy came down and fit for me until mother came up. i am all rite now and tomorow i can go in swiming. it was the babys berthday today. he was just 1 year old. he is a auful fat little baby, when i was sick mother wood let him sit on the bed.

July 8. brite and fair. i went in swimming today. the water was jest as warm as if it came out of the kittle.

next monday i am going bull froging with Cawcaw Harding.

July 9. brite and fair, nothing today but church.

July 10. me and Cawcaw had a prety good time today. we cougt 3 dozen bull frogs legs. we got sum old busters. it is auful funny to catch them. they will bite a bare hook, so we swing the hook by them and they gump for it and then they kick and almost tern rong side out trying to get of of the hook. then we grab them by the legs and whak their heads over the side of the bote and their inside comes out and sumtimes lots of hard water snales comes ratling out and sumtimes they has fishes and sumtimes other bull frogs or stripers. then we cut of there legs. me and Cawcaw always kill them ferst. sum fellers cut of there legs ferst, that is prety cruil i think. Cawcaw he thinks so two.

July 11. brite and fair. today i went in swiming up to sandy bottum. Whack and Boog and Puzzy were there and got to pluging green apples. Whack got behind a tree and jest as he peeked out Boog pluged a hard one and took Whack rite in the mouth. then Whack got mad and said he cood lick Boog and Puzzy together, so Boog and Puzzy piched in and had a good fite and punched time out of Whack. While i was waching them fite, sumbody tide gnots in my shert sleavs so tite that i coodent get them out so i had to go home without my shert on. it was prety lucky i had my jaket on.

July 12. Today i went up to Whacks and we et sum green currents with shugar on them and then et sum green apples and then we went in swimming down to sandy bottum. i dont feel very well tonite, i have got a bely ake.

July 13. i have been sick all day, mother made me take a big spoon full of caster oil.

July 14. i am beter today, it raned all day and tonite they was a thunder shower, it struck a tree in Gilman field.

July 15. i went up to Whacks agen today. i dident eat enny green apples or green currents you bet. Whack and Boog and Puzzy did and they give little Willie sum. they never have the bely ake. i never see such fellers.

July 16. i have got a velosipede, it ways 90 pounds. i have got so i can ride it down hill, last nite i was riding it up by Gim Odlins and it ran rite into a tree and i came of rite over it and scrached my hands and nocked the skin of my gnees. today was sunday and i coodent ride it but i set on it.

July 17. Hot as time today. Docter Gerrish and Docter Perry and J. Albert Clark have all got buly velossipedes, they have spring backs but mine is solid iron back and when i go over a bump or a stone it most ratles my teeth out. Beany he can ride two, but Pewt cant.

July 18. feerful hot.

July 19, 186- we fellers is going to have a swiming mach. they is going to be prises for the feller whitch can dive the best and for the feller whitch can swim the fastest and for the feller whitch can swim the furtherest under water and for the feller whitch can flote the best without wigling his arms and legs. i bet i will beat sum of the fellers. most of the fellers can beat me rassling or nocking of hats or running or gumping but i bet i will show them sumthing when we come to race in swiming. i practised today diving until my head aked feerful.

July 20. the race is to be next Wensday. They is Pewt and Beany and Fatty Gilman and Fatty Melcher. Boog and Whack and Puzzy was going to race but they wanted to have it at sandy bottum and we fellers wanted to have the diving mach at the oak and the swiming under water at the gravil becaus it is wider there, and so they was mad and woodent come in. Ennyway sandy bottum isent wide enuf and you cant tell whether a feller is swiming one foot on bottum. today i went in 7 times. ferst i practised swiming fast bullfrog fashion. next i practised side stroak next i practised swiming under water. i swum 5 times acros at the gravil. then i practised floteing, but i cant flote without keeping my hands moving. ferst my feet sink and when i get straight up and down my head goes under. then i div until my head aked like time agen. i feel prety tired tonite.

July 21. rany as time. i only went in swiming 2 times today and i dident dive enny. i only practised swiming fast and floteing. i coodent flote. in every boys book of sports and amuzements it says throw yourself on your back and throw your head back and hold your breth and you will not drownd until asistance reeches you. so i tride it today but i coodent hold my breth more than 1 minit and as soon as i let out my breth down i went unless i kep my hands moving. so what the man whitch rote that book said aint so unless asistance comes in 1 minit.

July 22. brite and fair and hot as time. Pewt thinks he is going to beat me swiming. i gess he will find out.

July 23. today was sunday and i coodent practise swiming or diving, darn it.

July 24. brite and fair. i only went in swiming 2 times today, once this morning and once this afternoon, but i staid in all the morning and all the afternoon so i coodent go in more then 2 times. the race is day after tomorow.

July 25. brite and fair. today we went up to Pewts and we aranged about the prises. Pewt was to give the prises. the prise for swiming fast was a bag of erly apples from Pewts garden. the prise for swiming under water was a gewsharp and the prise for the best diver was a cain fishing pole and the prise for floteing was a arrow rifle. we all give 5 cents eech to buy the cain pole. the gewsharp was one whitch Pewt had and the arrow rifle Pewt had made. So Pewt he said as long as he give 2 of the prises he was to have the say about whitch beat.

July 26. brite and fair. the fellers plaid a meen trick on me today. the meenist i ever see. i wont ever speak to enny of them agen. this morning we had the race. ferst we had the fast race. we started at the oak and swum down to the gravil. i was as far as from here to Beanys house ahead. so i got the apples. Fatty Melcher was next and Pewt was next and Beany and Fatty Gilman got tired and went ashore. next we had the floteing mach. Fatty Gilman floted the longest and then Beany becaus he was fat two and then Pewt and then Fatty Melcher and then me. i was the wirst and the fellers all howled at me. so Fatty Gilman he got the arrow rifle. i dont cair. then we went back to the oak to have the diving mach.

after we had div Beany and Fatty Melcher they said i div the best and Pewt and Fatty Gilman said Pewt div the best. then Pewt giv himself the prise becaus he had the say. i was prety mad. then we went down to the gravil to have the swiming under water mach so i went ferst and i swum from the going in place on Moltons field to the elm tree on old Nat Gilmans side and when i come up and looked round they wasent enny feller ennywhere. so i swum back prety lively and my close was gone and the apples and the gewsharp and the fellers two. so i dident know what to do. i thougt they had hid the close and i hunted in the buches but i dident find them. so i wated a long time and bimeby i heard sum oars and i looked and i saw a bote with a feller and 2 girls, so i coodent holler and i hid behind a tree. so they went by and then i come out and i walked back to the oak and when i got there i found sum girls picking dasies and i lay down behind the fence and just then a hornet stung me 2 times and i yelled and gumped rite up and danced round before i thougt and then i see them and i hipered back to the gravil, they hipered two the other way you bet. well i set there in the shade for a long time until i got kind of cold and then i set in the sun. i thougt sum of the fellers wood come in swiming, but nobody come. i knowed if i wated til dark i cood get home all rite, only i wood get a licking for scaring the folks most to deth for they wood think i was drownded. well jest then i heard sum fellers talking up by the oak and i went up and there was Potter Goram and Chick Chickering. they had been fishing and had cougt sum buly pikeril. well i holered to them and they come down where i was and i told them about the meen trick the fellers had plaid on me and Potter he said he wood go home for sum close and he give me his jaket and then he hipered acres the field and me and Chick began to fish and i cougt a pirch and a eal and Chick he cougt

2 roach. then Potter he come back with my best close and so i coodent fish enny more. so i went home in my best close. when i went by Pewts he holered Plupy has got on his best close. i dident say ennything. so when i got home mother asked me about it and i told her, it want telltaily eether. so mother she told me to go up to Pewts for my close and i said if Pewt took them he cood bring them back and Beany and Fatty two. so at super father he asked me why i had got on my best close and i told him and he said if Pewt dident bring those close back in about 5 minits he wood go up and boot him down to our house and back agen and jest then Mister Purington came into the yard holding Pewt by the ear. Pewt he had the close and Mister Purington he nocked at the door and he asked for me and when i come to the door he made Pewt give me the close and then he told Pewt to tell me he was sorry for what he had done and Pewt he dident want to say it but Mister Purington most lifted Pewt of the ground by the ear and then Pewt he said he was sorry kind of mad like and Mister Purington lifted him up agen til Pewt he stood on his tip toes and his face was all onesided and his eyes all squinty and then he had to say it over agen polite. and then Mister Purington he led Pewt home all the way by the ear. i thougt i shood die. it sirved Pewt jest rite. father laffed when i told him how the hornet stung me and how the girls hipered.

July 27. brite and fair. Pewt cant go out of the yard today. i dident speak to Beany.

July 28. brite and fair. i am going with Potter and Chick Chickering instead of Pewt and Beany. we went butterflying today.

July 29. brite and fair. nothing to wright today.

July 30. thunder storm rite after church. i wish it had been rite before.

July 31. tonite a man come down to see father and said i had gumped up behind a fence without my close on and scart his girls. he was stoping at the beach and they come up to Mager Blakes hotel. well father called me in and i told the man all about it and bimeby he begun to laff and he said it was a prety meen trick on me and he shook hands with me and he was glad i dident do it a purpose only he was sorry i got stung.

Aug. 1. me and Potter and Chick went fishing. Chick fell of little river brige with his close on. Potter caugt a whacking snaping tirtle. he gave it to Sam Dire and he cut his head of after it was cut of it wood bite a stick. Sam says it wont die til the sun goes down. he says that if you cut a snake in 2 peaces it will come together agen and heel up and be as good as ever. me and Potter is going to try it.

Aug. 2. big thunder shower last nite. we all got up and lit lamps and set round in our nite sherts. we lit all the lamps we cood find so we coodent see the litening. father kept telling funny stories, but mother and Aunt Sarah was scart and told him he hadent aught to joke when enny minit he mite be struck by litening. father he said he dident beleave the litening wood strike him enny quicker for not being scart of it then it wood if he gumped and holered o lord every time it litened. well after a while it only litened way of and we went to bed.

Aug. 3. i havent spoke to Beany yet or to Pewt eether.

Aug. 4. this morning it was Friday. we have fish chowder Fridays. i dont like it and so i drink milk and father wanted the milkman to go down celler to try some of his vinegar. mother hangs the wash boiler and the tin pans and iron kittles in the celler way and when ennyone whitch is tall goes down celler he has to stupe down so not to nock down the pans and kittles. so father he was down celler and he holered for the milkman to come down and when he went down he hit his head aginst the boiler and nocked it down and all the kittles and pans tumbled down on his head and went banging down into the celler and you never heard such a feerful noise. father was mad as time, but after the milkman was gone we all laffed as if we wood die. mother and Aunt Sarah had to set down they laffed so. mother said it made more noise then the thunder did last nite.

Aug. 5. me and Cawcaw Harding has got a new way of fishing for pikeril when we are in a bote. one of us padles the bote and the other skips for pikeril. when you try to pull a pikeril into a bote most half of the time he goes over the bote into the water, so when me and Cawcaw fishes when the feller which is skiping gets a bite he lets him have it a minit and the feller whitch is padling the bote padles towards the shore and then the feller whitch is skiping gumps rite out as soon as the water aint over his head and gives a big yank, and the pikeril goes saling into the field. sumtimes when it is woods the line gets tangled all up in a tree and we have to shin up the tree or cut it down to get the pikeril. we get prety wet but we dont cair. we always ring out our close when we get done fishing and they is most dry when we get home. today the bigest pikeril we caugt got up in a tree and we coodent shin up the tree and we coodent plug him down with rocks so we had to leeve him there. we got 12 pikeril. we are going monday.

Aug. 6. brite and fair. today after sunday school Beany he came over and we made up. this was the longest time i ever was mad with Beany. i am glad we aint mad enny more. father let me go to ride with Mister Watson and Beany this afternoon. we went down to the beach and took our lunchun. when we was coming home me and Beany got most asleep and our legs got asleep two, so Mister Watson he told us to get out and walk a little and we wood be all rite and when we got out he whiped up his horse and drove of lively and made me and Beany walk most a mile. we kep awake after that you bet. i had a good time.

Aug. 7, 186- clowdy but no rane. me and Cawcaw went fishing agen today in the bote ferst i padled and he skiped and then he padeled and i skiped. when we got up by the cove i got a bite and Cawcaw he padled the bote towards the shore and i gumped out lively and gumped into a deep place and went down way under. when i came up Cawcaw was nearly ded he laffed so. well i held onto my pole and swum to the shore it was only 3 stroaks and i sloshed up the bank and yanked that pikeril way into the buches. he was a big one. Cawcaw did it purpose. sumtime i am going to rock the bote sudding when Cawcaw is standing up skiping and he will go into the river kerswash.

Aug. 8. hot as time. me and Beany rung sum more doorbells tonite. we dident get cougt.

Aug. 9. brite and fair. Potter Goram can stuf birds, so they look jest like they was alive. he stufed a red winged blackbird so good that the cat et it and dide. and then Potter he skun the cat and stufed her. i can skin the cat on the horizondle bar, that is another way.

Aug. 10. me and Beany rung sum more doorbells tonite. we rung old Heads doorbell and then we tiptode round by the side of his house into Gim Ellersons yard and laid down behind the current bushes. well jest as old Head come piling out mad as time Pewt and Fatty Melcher come rite by and old Head grabed for them and Fatty he run and Pewt got cougt and old Head he jest lammed Pewt with his cain and Pewt holered he dident do it and old Head said he did and then he give Pewt sum good bats and sent him home balling. me and Beany most dide only we dident dass to laff out loud. jest then father come out to see what Pewt was holering about and he said what is the matter Orrin and Mister Head he said sum cussid boy has been ringing my door bell most every nite and i cougt him tonite and licked him good. and father he said who was it, and Mister Head he said it was Brad Puringtons boy, and father said i am glad it wasent my boy and mister Head he said i am glad two but i gess your boy woodent be meen enuf to ring doorbells and father he said i gess he woodent eether and then they went in and me and Beany we tiptode up Maple street and down town and then back home jest as if we had been down town all the time. that was a good one on Pewt. it made me think of the time Mister Watson Beanys father licked Beany when we rung his doorbell and he came to the door with a lamp and the wind blowed the lamp out and Mister Watson he bumped his head on the door.

Aug. 11. brite and fair. i cant help laffing every time i think of Pewt getting licked. it is a good one on Pewt.

Aug. 12. brite and fair. tonite me and Beany tride the same trick on Nipper. we saw Nip go down town and we rung Bill Greenleefs bell 2 times before Nip come back. we hid in old Ike Shutes porch and peeked out of a little window. Bill he come out and run round the side of the house and then he run up street and looked behind trees and fences and swoar terible. me and Beany near dide. he was so mad that he staid up til nearly 10 oh clock waching. we cood see him peeking out of the window and we dident dass to go home til after 10 oh clock and i got licked for being late. if Nipper had only come home when he had aught to Bill wood have cougt him and licked him and we wood have got home all rite. we will pay Nip for this.

Aug. 13. brite and fair. nothing but church today.

Aug. 14. brite and fair. i coodent go out of the yard today. Beany he come over and we are going to ring old man Hobbses door bell tomorow nite. old man Hobbs is Prisils uncle.

Aug. 15. brite and fair, and hot as time. tonite we rung old man Hobbses door bell 2 times. it was auful funny. the ferst time he come out kind of slow with a lamp. me and Beany were rite on the other side of the street laying down in the long grass. well he looked all round and walked out to the end of the piaza and then he went in mutering. bimeby we rung it agen and out he come prety lively but he dident catch us. if he was as lively as Bill Greenleef he wood have cougt us. well he went round the house and then old Missis Hobbs she came to the door and said what is it William, and he said it is some more of that Purington boys deviltry, and she said i wood speek to his father and old Hobbs he said he wood and then they went in. jest as we was going to ring the bell agen a man come walking quick down the street and went up to the door and rung the bell and jest as the bell rung old Hobbs opened the door quick and gumped out and grabed the man and said you rascul i have got you and the man said you old fool are you crasy and then old Hobbs he said i thougt it was that Purinton boy ringing my door bell and then the man went in the house and we wated til they had shet the door and we put for home and made sum sweet firn segars. tomorow old Hobbs is going to tell Pewts father. i never had so much fun in my life.

Aug. 16. brite and fair. today Pewt come down to the house and said where was you last nite and i said me and Beany was making sweet firn segars over to Beanys and i gave him 2 segars. then Pewt he said that old Hobbs come down to his house today and told his father he rung his doorbell 2 times and Pewt said he dident and his father said he dident beleeve him and was going to lick time out of him if he had and he did it. Pewt was prety mad and i was prety surprized you bet. this afternoon they was a thunder storm. after it was over we went fishing but dident get a bite.

Aug. 17. brite and fair. went up to Whacks this morning and Boog and Puzzy had 2 fites. neether licked becaus old miss Finton come out and stoped them. Boog got a bludy nose the second fite. in the afternoon i went fishing with Cawcaw. i dident get a chance to tip him over but we cougt 5 pikeril. tomorow nite me and Beany are going to ring sum doorbells.

Aug. 18. clowdy but no rane. jest the rite day to go fishing. i was going with Cawcaw but he was sick becaus he et to many apples up to Whacks. tonite Beany coodent go out of the yard becaus he dident split sum kindlings so we dident ring enny doorbells. it was a prety meen day. all the fun i had was going in swiming.

Aug. 19. prety hot today. i went in swiming 5 times. sumthing is the matter with my eyes i keep winking them all the time. father keeps saying stop batting your eyes. i gess it is becaus i keep opening my eyes under water to see things on bottum. father says if i dont stop it i shant go in swiming enny more.

Aug. 20. it raned this morning so hard that i dident have to go to church. buly.

Aug. 21. brite and fair. tonite me and Beany rung old Missis Sawyers bell. when she come out with the lamp we run into Pewts yard and then into Nat Weeks. she went in and come out agen with a shorl on and went rite over to mister Purintons and nocked at the door. we was near enuf to hear evrything. when Pewts father come to the door she said i think things has come to a prety pass if peeple cant keep there boy from trubling there nabors. and then Mr. Purinton Pewts father said what is the matter and Missis Sawyer she said your boy has been ringing my doorbell and Pewts father he said how do you know he did it and Missis Sawyer she said i see him run rite into your yard. and so Pewts father he come out and went round the yard but coodent find ennybody. so he said praps it was the Watson boy or the Shute boy and she said praps it was becaus she had heard they was prety bad boys. then Pewts father said it was a mersy if they dident both get into jale and she said she gessed the Shute boy was a trial to his father and mother and Pewts father he said he gessed the Watson boy was two. then he said if he was her he wood go rite down and see there fathers. when me and Beany heard that we clim over Nat Weeks fence esy and put for home. when we got there they was nobody in Beanys kichen and we went in esy and got the sweet firn and begun to make sweet firn segars. bimeby we heard old Missis Sawyer blabing to Beanys mother and she said she wood go in and see if Elly was in and when she come in Beany said mother jest see how many segars me and Plupy has made and he held up a lot that we made last week and she said you boys must have wirked a long time and Beany he said it takes a good deal of time to make so many and she went back looking prety pleased becaus she thougt Beany dident ring the old doorbell and she told old Missis Sawyer that we had been making sweet firn segars all the evening in the kitchin. so old Missis Sawyer went home kind of mad becaus it wasent me and Beany whitch rung her doorbell ennyway she thougt it wasent.

Aug. 22. brite and fair.

Aug. 23. brite and fair. tonite me and Pewt and Beany and Fatty Gilman and Fatty Melcher and Billy Swett and Gim Erly and lots of the fellers come up and plaid i spy the bull. one feller lays it and he shets his eyes at the gool and counts fifty and the rest of the fellers go and hide and when he has counted fifty he trys to find the fellers and tag his gool before they do. they is a stick leening agenst the gool and if one of the fellers can get to the gool ferst he can plug the stick as far as he can and the feller whitch is laying it has to run and get the stick and go back to the gool and leeve the stick there before he can find enny more fellers and if enny fellers has been cougt they can hide agen. so tonite we plaid it til nine oh clock and i had laid it most an hour when Pewt pluged the stick and hit old Bill Morril rite in the head jest as he came round the corner and he was mad as time and we put for home jest lively. Pewt dident meen to do it. Bill hadent aught to have been coming round the corner jest then ennyway. Bill told father they was the tufest set of boys in the naborhood he ever see. i was behind the current buches when Bill told father this and he showed father his old plug hat whitch was all dented in. father he said well Bill we usted to make things prety lively when we was boys. then he told Bill that he usted to ask his father if he cood go over and sleep with Gim Melcher and his father wood say yes, and Gim Melcher he wood ask his father if he cood go over and sleep with father and Gims father wood say yes, and they wood stay out all nite and raise time, and Gims father he wood think Gim was over to fathers house, and fathers father wood think father was over to Gims house and so they woodent get cougt. that wood be a prety good trick for me and Beany to try only father wood know two mutch. i gess that is the reason father finds out so mutch about me becaus he was prety tuf when he was a boy. i gess that is the reson why ministers boys is most always tuf becaus there fathers dont know how to find out what tuf things they do. i wish i was a ministers son so i cood be tuf and not get found out, only i wood have to go to church 3 times evry sunday.

Aug. 25. brite and fair. i wish i was ded. a feller might as well be ded as to be getting licked all time for nuthing. tonite me and Beany wated till it was dark and we saw Bill Greenlef go down town. then we tide a string to his doorbell and hiched the other end to old printer Smiths door on the other side of the street and hauled it tite. bimeby Bill he come back and went in the side door. then a man came by driving a horse and when the horse run agenst the string both doorbells rung before the string broak and out come Bill and old printer Smith. when they found they wasent ennyone there they was prety mad. Bill he run round looking behind fences and trees and old printer he swoar terible and went through Miss Sulivans and over to Nipper Browns and all round. me and Beany was hiding in Ike Shutes porch. bimeby they come back and talked. Bill said they must be 2 of them and old printer he said it was about time this thing was stoped and he was going to find out who did it if it took him all summer. well bimeby they went in to wate and see if ennyone rung there doorbells sum more. Bill he said he wood leeve his door open jest a little and old printer Smith he said he wood leeve his open jest a little two so he cood gump out and lam time out of the feller whitch rung his bell. well bimeby me and Beany crep out esy and hunted round til we found the string and we tide it agen as tite as we cood and then we crep back into the porch and peeked through the window. bimeby old mister Lyford come up the sidewalk and when he come to the string it gerked his old plug hat of and he picked it up and brushed it and then went of. bimeby a hack came by and when it hit the string both door bells gingled feerful and Bill and old printer Smith came hipering out as if they was hiched to the string. Bill went to gump of the side of the steps and he got the string round his leg and went fluking and then holered to old printer Smith that they was a string tide to his door bell and printer he holered back that they was one tide to his two. then they swoar and talked sum and jest then Pewts father come out and they said it was Pewt and old Missis Sawyer she come out and she said it was Pewt two. well then they begun to hunt and look behind trees and into doorways and me and Beany got prety scart and bimeby we opened the door esy and hipered round Ikes house and ran rite into old printer and he grabed us both by the neck and holered i have got the misable cusses and he draged us out to the lite and Bill and Brad said it is George Shutes boy and Irv Watsons boy and they shook us up lively. well old Missis Sawyer wanted them to take us to jale but Pewts father and Bill and printer said to take us down to our fathers and so printer held us by the neck and marched us down the street and Pewts father and Bill come along two and old Missis Sawyer she came taging along talking all the time that we was the wirst boys in town. we went down to fathers ferst and he come out and Bill he went over and called mister Watson. well he come over and they all went into the back yard and they told father about it and Missis Sawyer said she was going to have us arested and father he said if she wanted to arest me all rite but he wood get a lawyer and carry the case to the circus coart if it took evry cent he had and Mister Watson he said so two. and father he said he woodent have his boy distirbing his nabors and he wood lick me and make me beg evrybodys pardon, but it wasent merder or hyway robery to ring doorbells and if they wanted to arest me to sale rite in, and Mister Watson he said so two. then father and Mister Watson marched us up to old Hobbs and made us beg his pardon and old Hobbs told father we was the wirst boys in town and father aught to whale the life out of us, and then we went down to Pewts and had to beg his pardon for getting him a licking and then we went over to mister Heads and begged his pardon two. then father took me into the kichin and give me a licking for eech doorbell that we rung. he give me a good one for Missis Sawyer becaus she was a woman and he said we dident have enny bizness to plage a woman, and he give me a prety good one for Bill becaus Bill was a prety good feller, and he only hit me one lick for old Hobbs becaus he was mad at what old Hobbs said and he dident hit me a lick for mister Head becaus Pewt got licked for it and he said Pewt had aught to have been licked so many times when he dident that one licking one way or the other woodent make much diference. the wirst was when i had to beg Pewts pardon. i wood rather get 2 lickings.

Aug. 26, 186- Brite and fair. tonite i asked father about him and Gim Melcher staying out all nite and he laffed and said it was trew. then i asked him how menny times he did it and he said all the times he wanted to becaus his father thougt he was a beter boy then he was. well i asked him if i cood stay out all nite sum time and he said no. then he said i woodent dass to and i said i bet i wood. then he said i cood if i wanted to and then mother she said George are you crasy and he said no but he gessed after i had been out a while i wood be homesick. so after super i asked Beany and Beany he asked his father and he told his father what father said and bimeby Mister Watson Beanys father he said Beany cood stay out if i cood. so we are going to stay out Monday nite.

Aug. 27. brite and fair. nothing but church.

Aug. 28. rany as time. jest the luck. i coodent sleep enny last nite thinking about staying out all nite. ennyway i dident go to sleep til most morning and when i woke up it was raning hard, and it raned hard all day. it has stoped now. they wasent enny fun today.

Aug. 29. brite and fair. i am wrighting this in the morning becaus i shall be to bizzy tonite to wright ennything. i bet me and Beany will have sum fun. last nite father said they was a tiger got out of a circus and he kind of thougt it was somewhere in the Eddy woods. i aint afrade. Beany aint neether.

Aug. 30. brite and fair. i gess i wont try to stay out all nite agen. it aint enny fun. yesterday afternoon mother made me go to bed so i woodent be sleepy at nite and Beanys mother she did two. i coodent sleep and bimeby i got up and stuck my head out of the window and looked over to Beanys house and Beany he was looking out of his window and bimeby Potter and Cawcaw went by with their fish poles and you bet i wanted to go two, but i had to stay in my room. so Beany and i begun to holler acrost to each other and i made up this poitry about Beany,

fat pork and beens
thats what it meens
that Beanys got the belyake
from fat pork and beens.

and then Beany he made up this poitry about me,

Plupy Shute is meener than Pewt
and he is a prety meen galoot.

then mother made me go in a room on the other side of the house, but i coodent sleep and she let me get up at super time. when father come home he said the tiger had carrid of and et up a bull over to Kingston and he gessed he was coming this way, but i wasent scart. well after super i split my kindlings and me and Beany went down town. we went to doctor Derborns store and got sum soda water and Beany he paid for it. then we got sum goozeberries of old Si Smiths and i paid for them and then we went over to Beanys and got a lot of sweet firn segars and then we went down town agen. we went into stores and looked at things and we went down to the warf and then we went acrost to the raceway and went in swiming. it was kind of cold and we dident stay in very long. then it began to be dark and we went back to water street and staid in the stores til the nine oh clock bell rung and then we went back home. the folks was all setting on the front steps. so me and Beany set down two and bimeby the folks said they must go in and they all went in and shet the door. it made me feel lonesum when i herd them lock the door. it must be prety tuf on fellers whitch havent got enny home. then me and Beany went over to his house and set on the steps til his folks went in and shet the door and then we set on the fence under the gas lite and we herd Nat Weeks come home and mister Gewell and bimeby Si Smith shet up his store and then it begun to be loansum. so we went down as fer as the swamscot house and they was a lite in sum of the rooms and we set down on old Kellogs steps and talked. bimeby old Straton the gas man come round with a little ladder and clim up and put out the gas and then it was prety dark. then Beany he said less go up to Pewts and yowl like cats. so we went up into Pewts garden and we begun to yowl feerful like cats and bimeby Pewts father opened a window and holered scat you devils and jest then Nat Weeks he stuck his head out and he holered scat two. and then we kep still a minit and Pewts father said i wish there wasent a cussid cat alive and Nat Weeks he said so two and then they went to bed agen. bimeby we begun to yowl agen and then we yowled jest like cats fiting and Pewts father opened the window agen and pluged a club out into the yard and holered scat and then we kep still and we herd him tell Nat Weeks that he had got his gun loded and if he herd it go of he needent be sirprized. so you bet we dident yowl agen. so after Pewts father and Nat Weeks had gone to bed agen we clim over the fence esy and went of up towards Gilmans barn. Beany stumped me to go as fer as the barn and we was going there when i thougt of the tiger and told Beany about it. we wasent afrade but they wasent enny fun in going down to the barn so we went back down towards the high school yard and it was prety dark there and so we dident go down to set on the steps. bimeby it struck eleven oh clock. ferst the town clock and jest after it the factory bell an then we cood hear clocks striking in the houses on the street. i tell you it made me feel loansum. we coodent see enny lites in the houses, so we set on the steps and told stories and talked about the fellers and the girls. Beany said he gessed he wood mary Lizzie Tole, Ed Toles sister sum day. i bet he wont. then Beany he said when he was a man he wood by the club stable and have all the horses he wanted to drive, and i cood wirk for him if i dident get drunk [curiously enough, the first two statements in this prophecy came true] like most of the hostlers. i told him that i wasent going to wirk for ennybody for i was going to play in the band like Bruce Brigam, Scotty Brigams brother. bimeby we herd sum real cats yowling and it sounded sort of feerful. Cele read us a story when we was sick with the scarlet fever about a man whitch had a black cat and he got mad with her and cut out one eye. then he got mad with his wife and cut her throte and stuck her up in the chimny in the celler and pluged up the hole. bimeby the polisemen come to find out where his wife was and they hunted evry where in the house and stable and hen koop and evrywhere and bimeby they wanted to go into his celler. so the man he said all rite fellers come rite down and so the polisemen went down celler with him and he showed them all over the celler and they looked evrywhere and coodent find ennything and jest as they was going out they herd a feerful yowl and they stoped and lissened and it kept on yowling in the chimny and when they took a pickax and wanted to dig a hole in the chimny the man whitch killed his wife said they wasent ennything in the chimny for it hadent been opened for 1 hundred years, but they cut open the chimny and what do you gess they found. well they found his wife with her throte cut and a old black cat with 1 eye out setting on her showlder yowling. so they grabed the man and punched time out of him and they hung him to a lampost. well when Cele read that story to us we all was wirse for 3 days and Annie never got over it and when i hear a cat yowl i think of what the polisemen found in the chimny. so when i herd the cat yowling i told Beany that story and Beany he dident want to go of of my steps enny more. bimeby the town clock struck 12 oh clock and so it was morning and so we tost up to see whether Beany shood wait til i got in my house or i shood go over to Beanys to wait til Beany got into his house ferst. i lost jest as i always do and so i had to go over to Beanys and he tride the door and it was unlocked and so Beany he went in and i hipered acrost the road as quick as i cood and went in the back way. i wasent afrade only i wasent going to have Beany beat me in geting into bed. i went up stairs as esy as i cood but when i went by mothers room she said is that you Harry and i said yes and she said are you going out agen and i said no it is morning now and i am going to bed and she laffed and said good mornin. then i piled into bed and dident wake up til 10 oh clock. Beany dident get up til 12 oh clock. father saved a mans life today in Boston. he was a old man whitch tride to get on a train whitch had started and father saw he was going to tumble of and get killed and he run and grabed him and the old man tride to pull away and holered and the trane was going faster and father had to run and push the old man and he grabed him by the seet of his britches and give him a hist and piched him rite into the door of the car and then father he gumped of. evrybody said the old man wood be killed if it hadent been for father.

Aug. 31. i bet Beanys father never saved a mans life. i bet Pewts never did neether. i asked father if he xpected the old man to give him a good deel of mony for it or a gold wach, and father he said the conscenceless of having did a noble act is enuf reward. Gosh if i had saved a old mans life i wood have made him pay me. i wood have grabed him and said old man pay me 2 dolars or of goes your hind legs. i realy woodent let him drop but i wood have scart him til he give me 2 dolars. father he said that wood be hyway robery. i dont care.

Sept. 1. brite and fair. they was a peace in the Boston paper today about father. it said heroik rescu of a old man and it told about father saving the old mans life. lots of peeple spoke to father about it. father walked down town tonite 3 times. he most never goes down. father is going to take me to Boston tomorow if i behaive myself and dont do as i did before.

Sept. 2, 186- i had to get up feerful erly this morning. after brekfast me and father rode up to the depo in Joe Parmers hack. while we was wating for the trane Charles Talor and Charles Gray and all the fellers began to pich into father jest fun like and father got the best of them evry time. You cood here them holler about a mile. then the trane come and we piled in. evrybody knowed father and called him George and evrybody piched into him and he ansered back so that he made evrybody laff. that was the way it was all the way to Boston. when we got to Boston we went into a bird store and staid a while and then father took me out to see a house with a canon ball in it where the british had fired it in the revolution. then we went down to the custum house where father wirks and father took of his coat and put on a thin coat and put on sum cuffs made of pastbord and then he took out sum big books and begun to wright. he give me a sheet of yellow paper and a pensil and told me i cood draw sum pictures. when he come in one man holered hullo George what are you going to do with the boy, drownd him, and father he said no but i wood if he dident amount to more then you have, and then that man he shet up and a nother man he holered George have you saved enny more peeple and father he said no i had a chanse to but his name was Mudge and i let them hang him, and then that man he shet up. his name was Mudge two. bimeby a man come in with specks and side wiskers and sum papers and a squint eye, and he come up to fathers desk and father took the papers and wile he was wrighting i drawd the man with his specks and his old side wiskers and his squint eye. when father had fixed his papers the man said is that your boy mister Shute and he said yes and the man said can he draw and father said yes and he took the paper before i cood grab it and give it to the man and the man looked at it and begun to look mad and father said what is it and he showed it to father and then tore it up and went of mad. and father tirned red and asked me if i dident know more then that. then father he picked up all the peaces and we paisted them together and he showed it to the men and they all laffed and said i was a buster. bimeby a man come in and said that the naval oficer wanted to see father and father took the picture and went in. bimeby he came back and said the naval oficer jawed him and then he looked at the picture and laffed and said he wanted the picture and he took it and told father he had better shet that boy up. then it was dinner time and we went out and et dinner at a resterrant. i had meat and bread and coffy. after dinner we went back to the offise and a man come in and asked who was mister Shute and father said he was and the man said are you the man whitch put a old man on the trane at the depo and father said yes and i thougt the man wood give father a hundred dolars or a gold wach and father looked as if he thougt the man wood say noble man you have saved my fathers life, but the man looked mad and said well sir you did a prety smart thing to throw a helpless old man on to the rong trane and send him of 100 miles away from home and scart all his peeple most to deth becaus they thougt he was merdered and cost him 3 dolars to telegraf and stay all nite and if you dont know more then that you had beter soke your head. father he said what was the old fool trying to get on the trane for if he dident want to go on it, and the man he said he was trying to get of the trane and you woodent let him and the man holered so loud that evrybody cood hear him and shook his fist and went of swaring feerful. then Mr. Pope he said o what a fall was there my countrymen just like what was in the fourth reader and Mr. Davis he said immortal seezer ded and tirned to clay, that is in the fourth reader two. then all the men laffed and said the treat is on you George and father he laffed two and said he wood be cussed, and he said that is what a man got by not tending to his own bizness. tonites paper had a peace in it about father and said the old man whitch father put on the rong trane was going to be marrid and his girl got mad becaus he dident come and marrid another man whitch was there and the old man was going to sew father for braking up the mach. father said he bet Ben Ridwill and Jaky Howe rote it for the paper and he wood fix them.

Sept. 3. brite and fair. sunday today but father dident go to walk. he was prety cross two. Beany got sent out of sunday school for raising time. after he went out he clim up to the window and made up feerful faces at us. mister

Erl the suprintendunt was jest going to make a prayer and see us laffin and see Beany before Beany cood gump down and he grabed his cane and run out of the sunday school and chased Beany down to Gim Elersons. Beany cant come agen. i wish i was Beany.

Sept. 4. clowdy but no rane. school begins today,gosh

www.ingramcontent.com/pod-product-compliance
Lightning Source LLC
LaVergne TN
LVHW090615110826
845146LV00001B/404

* 9 7 9 8 8 8 0 9 1 1 3 6 3 *